Dutch Fred
IMMIGRANT

Carolyn Rohrbaugh

*To a special writers group friend
Janet
Carolyn Rohrbaugh*

 FriesenPress

Suite 300 - 990 Fort St
Victoria, BC, V8V 3K2
Canada

www.friesenpress.com

Copyright © 2017 by Carolyn Rohrbaugh
First Edition — 2017

All rights reserved.

This book is a work of fiction, but based on true events

No part of this publication may be reproduced in any form, or by any means, electronic or mechanical, including photocopying, recording, or any information browsing, storage, or retrieval system, without permission in writing from FriesenPress.

ISBN
978-1-5255-0368-9 (Hardcover)
978-1-5255-0369-6 (Paperback)
978-1-5255-0370-2 (eBook)

1. FICTION, BIOGRAPHICAL

Distributed to the trade by The Ingram Book Company

Table of Contents

ONE	THOUGHTS OF FREEDOM	1
TWO	SHIP OF MISERY	7
THREE	ARRIVAL	15
FOUR	THE JOB	25
FIVE	THEY FOUGHT FOR FREEDOM	35
SIX	CLEVELAND	39
SEVEN	MOVING ON	45
EIGHT	DECLARATION OF INTENT	51
NINE	IOWA	55
TEN	LAND AND NEIGHBORS	59
ELEVEN	A NEW FANGLED MACHINE	69
TWELVE	HARD TIMES	73
THIRTEEN	THE FACTS	81

AFTERWORD

ACKNOWLEDGEMENT

ONE
Thoughts of Freedom

The night brought thoughts of freedom in the New World as Fred lay by his wife's side watching her face in the dim light of the glowing embers.

His desire for freedom and a farm to own in America tortured him even before he married Wilhelmine and their child, **Marie** Sophie, was born. Fred reasoned that once he was married and settled down those thoughts would be put aside, but day after day he thought of nothing else. He would soon turn thirty-seven and felt he must fulfill his dream.

Fred watched Wilhelmine softly breathing. Her hair fell in ringlets across the pillow. He would love her always, but he knew that he must leave with or without her and Sophie. If she would not leave with him, Fred believed that when he arrived in America, he would have stories to convince her to leave Prussia and follow. Winter was upon them, and he would wait until spring to tell her, and that thought of telling her haunted him throughout the long winter.

Fred rose early each morning to chore. The animals were waiting for their morning portion of hay and oats. He threw feed to the chickens and fed the horse and pig. As he fed and milked the cow, his thoughts were consumed with freedom and a farm to own in America.

Although it was finally April, snow still covered the land, and field work could not be done. Fred stopped to listen to the migrating birds as they flew over and knew it was time to leave for America. He would tell Wilhelmine today that he was leaving.

He stepped into their meager one-room cabin, hung his coat on a peg, and set the pail of fresh milk on the table beside the bowl of mush Wilhelmine had prepared. The last piece of bread was divided between them, and there would be no more. The weevil-infested flour was gone, other supplies were scant, and few coins remained to purchase more. The sun was shining through the one small window warming him.

"Come sit with me, lie be frau," he said, as he moved closer to her chair, "Let's talk while Sophie sleeps. You mentioned that I have tossed about in my sleep lately. I must tell you why I am so restless." Fred chose his words carefully, hoping to convince her to take the journey to America with him.

"Wilhelmine, you know King Frederick William IV was declared insane and died soon after. William I is now King of Prussia. He is reorganizing and strengthening the army. The Legislature opposed him, and he appointed Otto von Bismarck prime minister to keep them under control. Bismarck wants Prussia to replace Austria as leader of the German States. Any opposition to their military program is being suppressed. I feel we will soon be at war and all men will be required to join their army. I am no longer young and cannot fight for something in which I do not believe. I want you and Sophie to travel to America with me, where we will live in freedom and not be afraid of war."

"I cannot leave this land and my parents. It will be too dangerous to travel so far with a small child. America could be more unsettled than Prussia. Please stay with me," she begged. "I am afraid for you to go so far away. I am sure the army will not want you as you are well into your thirties."

Fred looked deep into her eyes, "Wilhelmine, my age does not matter. Bismarck will make us all fight in his army. I have made up my mind; I will go with or without you and Sophie. If only you would come my dream would be fulfilled. We must leave before war breaks out and the border is closed."

Wilhelmine turned her head as a tear slid down her cheek. "Go to fulfill your dream. I love you, but I cannot leave my parents. They are old and need me."

Fred felt he should not leave his family, but the urge for a new life in America was stronger than the desire to stay.

He stepped back into the crisp morning and felt the burden had been lifted from his mind, but his heart was heavy as he stood in the quiet dawn and prayed Wilhelmine would change her mind. Later that day he hitched the horse to the wagon, helped Wilhelmine and Sophie step in, wrapped them in a deerskin blanket, and gently urged the horse on. They were going to her parents to ask if Wilhelmine and Sophie could reside with them until Fred was settled in America.

Her parents were excited to see them. It had been several weeks since they last visited. Wilhelmine's father, Johann Conrad Eilers, rushed to help her step down from the wagon and hold his only grandchild.

"Is something wrong?" Johann asked. He thought she seemed unusually quiet.

"No, Father, we have something to ask you."

"Come in, your mother will be happy to see you."

Fred helped Wilhelmine with her cape. They sat by the fire struggling with the words to ask her parents.

"I will get to the point, Father. Fred is leaving for America to find freedom and a farm to own. Sophie and I will need a place to stay until we are able to follow him."

Johann was a bit reserved, "What if you never see your wife and daughter again, Fred? Have you thought of this?"

Fred nodded and said, "We talked about it. They will come when I am settled."

"You will need silver to travel so far. There will be the expense of the ship passage and you will need supplies when you reach America."

Fred hesitated, "We will sell the farm, livestock, wagon, and butcher the hog. I will salt the pork for Wilhelmine and me to share. I have paid a good deal on the farm and should have a fair profit. I will take what is needed for ship passage and supplies on the trip. Wilhelmine will have the rest."

Johann took a pull on his pipe and looked Fred in the eye. "There won't be enough profit to support your wife and child for the rest of their lives. It will be best if she applies for a divorce. If you never return, she will have to marry another to support the child and herself." Fred was stunned; he had not thought of such a thing. He knew there would be hard decisions, but did not think this would be one of them.

Anna Marie glanced nervously at her husband. Johann hesitated as he returned Anna's glance and said, "Wilhelmine and Sophie can stay with us until Fred is settled in America." Anna smiled, and Johann knew she was pleased with his decision.

Wilhelmine was both sad and relieved, she said, "When Sophie and I arrive in America, we will remarry."

The next day sorrow filled their hearts as they applied for a divorce. Fred was hesitant as he applied for a permit to leave, but he must follow his dream. He was surprised to see how many people were in line wanting to leave Prussia and find a better life. The constable asked the man in front of Fred why he wanted to leave Prussia.

When the man answered, "To escape war," the constable stamped his paper, DENIED.

"Move on, you are not allowed to escape war."

Fred stepped up to the constable and when asked why he wanted to leave, he replied, "To work in America."

"What is your full name, date of birth, and do you have a family?" the man asked.

"I am Frederick Wilhelm Feldman, born March 19, 1827. I have a wife and daughter."

"Will you leave them behind?" the man asked.

Fred stammered as he answered, "When I find work, they will follow."

"What are their full names and birth dates?"

"My wife is Christine Wilhelmine Sophie Eilers Feldman, born March 27, 1844. My daughter is Marie Sophie Feldman, born November 29, 1863. We call her Sophie."

The constable stamped the paperwork and said, "This will be reviewed; return in a few days."

When Fred returned a few days later, no decision had yet been made. It was several weeks before he received word that he was granted a divorce and a permit to leave for America.

He hung posters around the village stating Frederick Wilhelm Feldman was selling his earthly possessions. One by one the horse, cow, chickens, wagon, and other items were sold.

Fred knew the farm could not be sold unless he presented it to August Kolbus, a ruthless real estate agent. August held all mortgages. When anyone wanted to sell their farm, August offered a low price telling them their land was worthless. He would not loan silver to anyone who wanted to buy land.

Fred sold his possessions for forty silver coins and his land to August for fifty silver coins. He paid his debt and was left with forty-five silver coins. A very small profit, but he had no choice.

There were so many immigrants leaving for America that the ruthless ship companies took advantage and charged thirty coins for passage tickets. After Fred purchased passage on the

Bremerhaven, from the port of Bremen to Pennsylvania, only fifteen silver coins remained. Fred and Wilhelmine discussed the amount each would need to survive. He would use two coins for supplies on the ship and three coins to purchase supplies in America, leaving the last ten silver coins for Wilhelmine and Sophie.

Fred emptied the small trunk that held their linens and filled it with dried fruit, salted pork, and his few possessions. He purchased an extra pair of boots and trousers, using three of the silver coins. Only two coins remained for him. He knew they would not be enough, but he would find work in America. The last item placed into his trunk was his knife.

The Bremerhaven would not leave until August. Fred would spend those last weeks with his family. Sophie was a pleasant child and Fred had second thoughts about leaving, but he knew he would not be happy if he stayed in Prussia. He must fulfill his dream.

The days slipped away and then it was time to leave. The night before he left, Fred and Wilhelmine lay together and discussed the future.

"Please come with me," he begged.

Wilhelmine sobbed as she whispered, "I love you, but I must stay with my parents."

Fred wondered if he would ever see her or hold her next to him again. Their tears intermingled as they made love for the last time.

TWO
Ship of Misery

The day of departure had arrived. Fred and Wilhelmine spoke of their love for one another as they embraced.

"I pray we will be together again. Take care of Sophie and keep her safe." He left, but turned one last time to bid them farewell.

Fred had never seen a ship before and to his surprise it seemed quite small for such a long voyage. The ship looked to be about one hundred and fifty feet in length and he guessed it was only thirty feet wide. Two hundred men, women, and children waited to board the ship. Fred held his passage ticket that stated:

Passage Record for Friedr Wilh Feldman:

Record id:	239128	Purpose:	Staying in America
Gender:	Male	Native Country:	Prussia
Age:	37 years	Embarkation port:	Bremen
Approx. birth year:	1827	Travel compartment:	Steerage
Occupation:	Farmer	Ship name:	*Bremerhaven*
Destination:	Pennsylvania	Date of arrival:	September 12, 1864

All were handed a list of instructions stating single men were to be berthed in the bow section and single women in the stern, separated by the married couples' section. Single men and women were not allowed to mingle or speak to one another on the ship. Single women were to be locked in their quarters at night.

1. Passengers shall rise at 7 a.m., at which time the fires for cooking shall be lighted.
2. All immigrants, except the sick, are to be dressed, beds rolled up, and the deck properly swept before breakfast; this is at 8 a.m.
3. Dinner at 1 p.m. and supper at 6 p.m.
4. Fires out at 7 p.m. and in bed by 10:00 p.m.
5. Swearing, immoral conduct, fighting, gambling, or drunkenness will not be allowed.

Each person's berth was very small. Three berths were stacked one above the other. They were three feet wide and only five feet in length. Accommodations consisted of that small berth, a supply of dried herring, and three meager meals a day.

Dinner tables were constructed to be hung from the timbers after each meal to allow floor space, but the seats were not fastened down and were often thrown about during a storm. Much of the space below deck was taken up by cargo, making conditions cramped. The deck above was crowded with people trying to walk and stretch their legs.

A health check had been required before departure, but many people were able to hide their illness from the inspector. It wasn't long before scarlet fever, typhoid fever, diphtheria, and tuberculosis spread around the ship. Diseases were exacerbated by damp and stagnant conditions below deck. Some were preyed upon by the sapping heat on deck. Young children were the most susceptible to the miserable conditions aboard ship, and many would not survive the voyage.

The first days of the trip were pleasant enough and passengers were able to spend time on deck, but then the weather changed. The ship pitched and tossed about, forcing the immigrants to stay below deck. Hatches were locked to prevent water from rushing into the living quarters below. Still, the water came in. Passengers who smoked lit phosphorous matches for a moment of light, but the matches were quickly extinguished for fear of fire, leaving everyone in darkness for days.

Day after day the immigrants were forced to stay below deck. Many were seasick from the tossing of the ship. Vomit and feces filled the water in which they stood. Misery spread throughout the ship.

Fred was wrenched with seasickness and could not venture from his berth. His short, restless sleep was filled with dreams of Wilhelmine and Sophie. He missed them, but knew it was best that they had stayed in Prussia. Wilhelmine had been right; the trip was too difficult for a small child.

With each roll of the ship, people were thrown from their bunks, often being hurled to the opposite side of the ship. Children were in danger of being crushed by the adults. Water poured through the deck, soaking bedding, and standing knee deep on the floor. Food could not be cooked nor lanterns lit. Two hundred people were confined to their bunks in darkness. Women screamed and children cried as the ship rolled and tossed violently. Any loose objects were hurled into other bunks battering men, women, and children. Passengers lay in sleeping places so narrow they could not move. No privacy existed, and the stench was unbearable. Sick and dispirited they huddled together in darkness, without fresh air, wallowing in filth. Washing clothing or body was not allowed as there was hardly sufficient water for cooking and drinking. They lived without food, a doctor's care or medicine, and died without hearing God's word. Many bodies were tossed into the ocean without ceremony.

Unscrupulous men plundered trunks robbing the people of food, coins, and other valuables.

Since crew members were suspected to be the culprits, it did no good to complain to the captain.

Fred hid his coins in his boot and kept close watch of his trunk. He began to wonder if going to America was worth all this turmoil.

After many days of misery and discontent, the tossing of the ship subsided. A man bunking below Fred found the strength to stumble up to the deck.

"The sun is shining and the seas are calm. Come to the deck for renewal," he shouted.

Fred staggered to the deck and found a sunny place in which to absorb the sun's warmth. For the rest of the journey he returned to the same place and watched the immigrants settling into a daily routine. Some were just strolling, some still purging over the side, and others were too sick to stand. Fred watched as a curious young lad found a rope attached to the railing and began swinging out over the ocean and back, to offset his boredom. Out and back, out and back, until he lost his grip and fell to his death in the cold, dark ocean. His mother approached as he slipped from the rope. Screeching an ear piercing wail, she attempted to follow her son, but the father held her back as she sobbed uncontrollably. They both watched as the boy sank out of sight and his cap floated into the distance. Nothing could be done and the ship continued on its way.

The days were filled with sorrow, and the captain put very little effort into comforting the immigrants. Fred tried to put the misery out of his mind . . . to no avail. On one occasion he watched a man bring his sick wife and child on deck for fresh air, but the baby was already dead and his wife died while Fred watched. That afternoon the man wept as the makeshift coffins were slid into the ocean. A schoolmaster said a prayer and read from the Bible for the woman and child and another woman, whose body was also dropped into the ocean, but without coffin or timber.

Without being asked, the schoolmaster gathered the children along the ship's wall and commenced teaching English. Fred slid close and listened. He knew he would have to speak English when he arrived in America. On occasion he dozed through the lessons, but he was able to learn many words which would prove to be a great help to him. A single woman sat beside him to learn English, but they did not speak to each other, since it was not allowed.

Fred would help the captain with chores. One day he helped pull a dolphin onto the deck. The dolphin would feed the immigrants for several days.

The ship owners brought a printing press on board and asked those who could write to contribute poems, stories, or letters to the editor. The ship's speed, current position, and expected date of arrival were also published.

> These letters have been contributed by passengers and master of the ship:
>
> Our daughter, Isabelle, was sick for three days. She died two days ago. Jessie
>
> Food and possessions were stolen from our trunk. The captain did nothing about it. Evan
>
> The class of immigrants aboard this ship appears to be above average. Your arrival will be a welcome addition to America.
>
> I.C. Hilken, Master of the Bremerhaven
>
> We are traveling at 4 knots and it will be several weeks before we arrive in America.
>
> I.C. Hilken, Master of the Bremerhaven

Many immigrants were unhappy with life on the ship and banned together to write a letter discouraging others from making the dreadful trip to America. The letter was put into a bottle and thrown into the ocean with the hope it would reach land and be found. The letter read:

August 16, 1864

> We are bound for America on the Bremerhaven. There were two hundred men, women, and children on board when the voyage began. Many have died. We wish to let the world know we are receiving inhumane treatment aboard this ship. Provisions are not fit for the worst convict. The food is scant, rancid and half-cooked. The bread could be made into putty or marbles for the boys. We want to deter immigration through any agent. Sickness, unsanitary conditions, and death prevail. We regret having made the decision to travel to America.
>
> Passengers of the Bremerhaven

Each day Fred watched as sickness and sorrow took its toll. On one occasion a man sat down beside him.

"Do you have a family with you?" he asked.

Fred stared into the man's eyes and wondered if his intentions could be to rob him.

The man continued talking. "Myself, my wife, and our two children, age's eight and six, left Prussia for freedom in America. We felt we could start a new life, but we should have stayed in Prussia. All three are dead of the fever and I am alone. It would have been more humane to die in war than on this god-forsaken ship."

Fred did not have words to help the man and did not respond. The man stood, slowly strolled to the railing, hesitated a moment, and leaped over the side to his death.

A passenger, out for a daily stroll, tripped on another man's foot and was arrested for drunkenness. He was taken to the captain who showed no mercy. The passenger declared that he had not had a glass of ale, but the captain sentenced him to pay a fine and spend one week in the hold.

Meals furnished by the ship's owners were scant, but when the ocean was calm the crew set fireplaces on either side of the foredeck. Those who brought provisions were able to cook at the fireplaces. The fire was contained in a wooden case, lined with bricks and confined by two or three iron bars. From morning to evening the fireplaces were surrounded by men and women attempting to cook griddle-cakes that were mostly burnt and covered with smoke. The fireplaces were scenes of endless quarrels. It was impossible for each person to remain close enough to the fireplaces to watch their cakes. Those who could shove their way to the front took the unburnt cakes, leaving the burnt ones to be fought over.

Cautiously, Fred would slip unseen to the hold to eat his dried fruit and salted pork. He worried that his supplies would be gone before reaching America and rationed them carefully. Each time Fred opened his trunk he reached to the bottom to feel if his knife was still hidden among his possessions. The knife was the most valuable item that he was carrying to the New World and the most difficult to replace. He needed it to hunt and defend himself.

He listened to stories of those remembering their homeland. He heard that farmers, carpenters, tailors, merchants, bakers, shoemakers, bricklayers, and professionals from many countries were traveling to America hoping for a better life.

At night Fred dreamed of Wilhelmine and Sophie. He wondered if he would ever see them again. Wilhelmine was not a strong person and he felt she would never survive this continuous nightmare of suffering.

THREE
Arrival

One morning Fred woke from a deep sleep and felt a soft breeze blowing through the ship. A ray of morning sun was shining through the door that led to the deck. This had not happened since their departure. He was confused and found it hard to understand. He crept quietly up the narrow stairs and stepped onto the deck where a young man stood with the sun shining on his back.

"We have changed directions. What does that mean?" the young man asked.

Fred looked toward the horizon and began to smile. Pointing west, he said, "There are gulls in the air; land is near."

Dancing with joy, they began to yell at the top of their voices. "Land . . . land is on the horizon." People poured onto the deck. Fred gazed at the speck of land in the distance. Surely this was the end of their misery.

Officers announced that the ship would dock in America the next day, and all would have to do their part to clean the ship today. Fred began to clean the deck; it would make the day go faster, and he wanted to watch the land come closer. His eyes were fixed on the dot of land that would become his home. If only Wilhelmine and Sophie were with him.

At days end the sun set over the bow of the ship, as if leading the way to America. As he watched the sunset, Fred pondered the events of the voyage. He thought of the people who had perished, those who had lost their children or spouse, the boy who had lost his grip on the rope, and the man who had joined his wife and children in the ocean. They would not see the land on the horizon. His thoughts went to the schoolmaster who had taught him the only English he knew. Fred was thankful that the schoolmaster read from the Bible for so many who had died, especially the lady whose body was dropped into the ocean without coffin or timber.

His new life was about to begin. He shivered as the wind blew, pushing the ship closer to America.

Fred sat on the deck at his favorite place . . . well into the night. The sky was black and clear. The moon reflected over the ocean beckoning the ship to America. The stars twinkled as if announcing the new life that lay ahead. Somehow memories of the past several weeks seemed to fade away and Fred knew he would find a new happiness.

When he finally went to his cot, his sleep was restless. The faces of the immigrants who traveled on that ship haunted him. He dreamed of Wilhelmine and Sophie. The ship seemed to toss as in a violent storm, but when he woke the sun was rising and land was so close he could smell the grass and trees and hear the gulls screeching in the distance.

As Fred stood watching the ship pull into port, the woman who had sat with him to learn from the schoolmaster stepped up beside him.

"Where will you go when we are off this ship?" she asked.

"I am a farmer and I will find land to till and grow crops. That is all I know. What will you do?" he asked.

"My sister lives in New York and she will be waiting for me." They stood together while the ship pulled close to shore. She left before he could ask her name.

The people chattered with excitement. It was almost unbelievable that they would soon step off this ship of misery into America.

Fred could not take his eyes from the land that lay ahead. Slowly, they passed the wreckage of a ship that lay splintered on the rocks. His heart was heavy as he wondered if its passengers had perished so close to their destination.

Fred felt confused and alone. He took a ship steward's arm and asked, "Where are we? What is the date, and how did that ship wreck upon the rocks?"

"This is the port of Baltimore and it is September 12, 1864. We have traveled for more than one month. That ship hit upon the rocks and sank due to the stupidity of the pilot. Many ships have sunk. Three years ago the Anglo-Saxon was lost at sea and the Norwegian was lost in 1863. The Bohemian struck rocks off the coast of Maine and sank before the immigrants could swim to shore."

Fred pondered what the steward told him and asked, "Is this Pennsylvania?"

"No, this is Baltimore, Maryland."

"My passenger record states that I would land in Pennsylvania. I was told there are farms to buy there."

"You can take the train to Philadelphia, Pennsylvania. It is not far from here," the steward replied.

Fred knew the train trip would cost coins, but he was determined to buy land and felt he must go to Pennsylvania.

The ship was tied to the dock, but the plank was not lowered. Everyone demanded to know why they were not being let off this ship of misery.

The captain held his arms up for quiet, "You will not be let off this ship until tomorrow when the health officer arrives to examine each one of you." Discontent prevailed, but nothing could be done. The night seemed longer than any other on the ship.

The next day the passengers left the ship and were sent to Dr. Hobbs, Health Officer. Each person was given a number in the order they were to be examined. Hobbs was a short man with frown lines defining his disposition. He was tired of looking into people's mouths and didn't care what color their nails were or if mucus ran from their nose. He didn't care if they coughed, as long as they didn't cough on him. It was just a job and one he was tired of doing.

When Fred stepped up to be examined Hobbs stated, "You are number 135. What is your name?"

"I am Frederick Wilhelm Feldman."

Hobbs wrote his name as Fried^k Wilh. Feldman.

"That is not right," Fred stated

"It is an abbreviation," Hobbs stated angrily.

Fred did not understand and moved away as soon as he was examined. After being examined, each person was directed to the baths. Men were sent in one direction, women and children in another. The women and children cried. They were afraid they would never see their husbands and fathers again.

"This way . . . this way," they were directed. Fear engulfed the men as they were led away from their families to the unknown. They were led down a long, narrow hall to a dingy, dimly lit room, where they were told to set their boots in a row, hang their clothes on hooks, and shower. Fred looked around to see if anyone was watching, then reached into his boot, withdrew his coins, and held them tight while he showered. Their clothes were still dirty, but it was a relief to wash the month of stench from their bodies.

After showering they were directed to a line where government officials asked their names and there they wrote Fred's name the same as Hobbs had written it. This time Fred did not mention the spelling.

"What is your destination?" the official asked. Fred didn't know what that was, but the person ahead of him had answered, 'Ohio' and that was what Fred answered.

Another stern man instructed them to follow the arrows painted on the floor to find their wives, children and trunks.

A man shouted and waved his hand pointing toward lines of government workers. "This line is to exchange money; this one to seek directions and this one to find employment. You can purchase a train ticket here. Spend the night on the floor if you wish, but move on tomorrow."

The officials warned them about thieves and opportunists who were hanging around the harbor waiting to prey on the ill-informed and desperate people arriving in the country. One of the officials told the immigrants that the culprits would try to sell them farms that did not exist. They will steal your money and lead you to the unknown. You will not find your dreams or jobs.

Fred approached an official and asked, "Who will tell me about work?" He was directed to a line where a clerk asked what work he was capable of doing.

"I am a farmer," he answered.

He was handed a list which he could not read and was worthless to him. The maps that hung on the walls were of little use. He was confused and could not understand most of what he was told. He did manage to understand that he should find the weight master. Each immigrant would point out his trunk and receive a certificate of weight. After claiming his trunk Fred found a place on the floor to spend the night.

That night as he opened the trunk, his thoughts went to the day that he had removed Wilhelmine's linens and placed his food and possessions inside; it seemed so long ago. The salted pork and dried fruit were nearly gone. He knew he must find a job soon.

He had not anticipated the feeling of depression, not knowing where to go, or what he should do. How would he find the train to take him to Pennsylvania and how would he find land to farm? He did not know what was north, south, east or west. Confusion filled his mind as he drifted off to sleep.

The next day he returned to the government official and asked directions to the train. The man pointed in a direction and told him the train was just over the hill.

He said, "If you have silver coins you should exchange them for American dollars."

Fred found an out-of-the-way place, retrieved the coins from his boot and returned to the official. After the exchange was made, he had several paper dollars, but he did not know their value.

Fred walked over the hill, purchased a train ticket and took the short trip to Philadelphia. When he stepped off the train he asked a stranger where he could find work.

The man replied, "There are no jobs in Philadelphia, but if you cross the river you might find a job at Castle Garden Immigrant Station on Manhattan Island. There is a tenement called The New Mission House on Cross Street where you will be able to rent a room."

It was dusk when the ferry took him across the river to Manhattan Island. Confused and alone, Fred saw people walking and followed them, hoping they would lead him to The New Mission House. No one seemed to know where they were going, but Fred was encouraged by the lights in the distance.

A man asked Fred to join the army. It made Fred angry and he shoved him aside.

"Why do you ask such a question? I could have been in the army in Prussia." Fred was sure this was one of the unscrupulous men about whom they had been warned.

Fred ran toward the lights to get away from the man and came to an intersection. At the center of the intersection was a triangular building. People were singing and dancing in the street, buildings were crumbling to the ground, filth was everywhere and the stench was unbearable.

He met a drunken man who slurred, "Welcome to Five Points where every species of vice exists."

Fred wanted away from this filthy place and asked the man where he could find "The New Mission House."

The drunken man laughed and pointed down the street, "You will find whatever you want down there."

Fred walked in the direction the man had pointed until he saw a sign that read, "The New Mission House." He stepped into a dimly lit, dingy, in-need-of-repair lobby.

"Need a room?" a figure behind the desk asked.

Fred nodded and asked how much it would cost.

"Forty cents for seven nights," the man replied.

Fred held out a paper dollar. He didn't know its value, but the clerk gave him several dollars and coins in return.

The man pointed to the top of the stairs and said, "Your room is the first door around the corner." The gray-haired man was straight-faced and as unpleasant as everyone Fred had met since arriving in America.

Upon opening the door Fred found a room so depressing that he would have left if exhaustion had not overtaken him. Roaches scurried across the floor leaving lines in the dust. The walls were spotted with what looked like blood and plaster was falling from the ceiling. A rusty medal bed held a soiled mattress with a torn and filthy blanket thrown over it. This was worse than the ship. Fred knew he must find a way to leave this place.

The next morning he ventured into the street where people milled about.

He stepped toward a gentleman and asked, "What is this place?"

The man answered, "This is Five Points, a slum filled with prostitution, crime, and disease. Immigrants are over-running this place. It is a breeding ground for disease, murder, and gangs. Last month a small girl living in a room with twenty-five people was stabbed to death for a penny she had begged."

"Why do you stay?" Fred inquired.

"We don't know where to go, we don't have enough money to leave, and there are no jobs for men. Women can enter into prostitution, but they risk being murdered. We feel safe from the war here, but staying in Prussia would have been better than this."

Fred was shocked and said, "I didn't realize there was a war here in America."

"Yes," the man replied, "It is called the Civil War. The states are fighting against each other."

"Tell me of this war. Why do they fight?" Fred asked.

The man knew little of the events of the war, but answered, "I believe they are fighting for freedom."

Fred returned to his room and sobbed. His desire was to return to Prussia. Wasn't America already the land of freedom? He remained in his room and thought of this insufferable place, the war, Wilhelmine, and Sophie until he fell into a troubled sleep.

When he woke he stared into the broken piece of mirror that hung on the wall above the dirty and cracked wash basin. His eyes were swollen and red, his face pale and ashen.

"I will find work and a way to leave this hellhole," he thought. "I did not endure the rigors of the journey to America to die in this slum." He stepped into the hall and saw a woman lying on the steps. Fred reached to touch her and knew death had taken her.

"Help," he called, as he made his way past her to the man at the desk. "There is a dead woman lying on the steps."

The man shrugged and said, "Just another prostitute, when will they learn? Someone will move her."

Stunned by the man's frivolous attitude, Fred ran into the street. Approaching the same man he had seen the day before, he said, "A dead woman is on the steps of the Mission House!"

The man shrugged and answered, "Just another prostitute."

Fred realized these people's hearts had become cold. Life here was meaningless to all who stayed in this place of abomination and he was determined to leave.

Fred noticed the street was lined with breweries filled with people drinking and fighting. He wondered if he might be able to find a job in one of the breweries. Coultard's Brewery, the Old Brewery, and Leopold's Brewery were all on Mulberry Street. Nicholas Bayard's slaughterhouse sat at the end of Mulberry Street thus nicknaming the street, "Slaughterhouse Street."

Fred smelled a vile odor and asked a man what caused the stench.

The man told him, "The smell comes from a pond, named the Collect Pond. It is a body of spring fed water that covers several acres and is very deep. Businesses are draining their sewage into the pond, causing the vile odor. It overflows constantly, covering the streets with sewage, and making them wet and slippery. Houses are shifting off their foundations. It is nearly impossible to walk on these streets; there are no jobs for men, and women have become prostitutes. These conditions have turned many men to drinking and fighting."

FOUR
The Job

Entering Coultard's Brewery, Fred pushed his way to the bar and asked if it would be possible to speak to the owner. The man behind the bar pointed to a tall, middle-aged man, sitting with a woman and drinking ale.

Fred approached the man and said, "Sir, I understand you are the owner of this establishment." The man glanced up and nodded.

"I am Frederick Wilhelm Feldman and I would like a job."

The man laughed. "There are no jobs here. What do you think you could do?"

"I am a farmer and I am strong. I will do anything you ask of me." At that moment a chair flew over their heads and a bottle crashed to the floor.

"Well, I am Mr. Coultard; if you can break up that fight over there, and throw the men out, I will hire you to keep the peace."

Fred was not a fighting man, but he needed that job. He strolled over to the drunken men and put a hand on each man's shoulder. The men were surprised that anyone would interfere and stopped to see who was so brave.

"Who the hell are you?" one of the men retorted as he threw a blow at Fred.

Anticipating such a move, Fred ducked and quickly grabbed the man by the shirt, throwing him through the door and into the street. Fred turned to the other man, who wasn't about to be thrown into the sludge covered street. He left, confused and muttering.

Fred told the men, "There will be no fighting in this brewery! I am Frederick Wilhelm Feldman and you will answer to me if you fight."

A policeman had been passing by and stopped to watch as Fred threw the man into the street.

Mr. Coultard stood to shake Fred's hand. "You will be my strong man and I will pay you fifty cents a week plus meals. You can start tonight." Fred did not know how much fifty cents was, but he would save his dollars to leave this place.

Fred was shocked to see all the evil happenings in that brewery. He watched as a man tried to persuade a prostitute to leave with him, but she was already with another man. The men fought and Fred threw them out of the brewery.

"Why do you think you can throw us out?" one of the men asked.

"I was hired by Mr. Coultard to keep the peace." Before Fred could get another word out, the man hit him so hard that he staggered backwards and fell to the floor. The man tried to kick him, but Fred caught him around the ankles and pulled him down.

Again Fred heard, "Who the hell are you?"

"I am Frederick Wilhelm Feldman and you will answer to me if you fight in this brewery." As he dragged the man out of the brewery, he noticed the same policeman watching. Finally, Fred walked over to the policeman and introduced himself.

"I am Frederick Wilhelm Feldman. I have noticed you watching each time I throw men out of the brewery."

The policeman laughed and shook Fred's hand. "I am Patrick O' Riley and it is an unusual sight to see men being thrown out of the brewery." Patrick was a short, red-haired Irishman. His black uniform was covered with dust and dirt and he had no weapon.

Some men desired certain prostitutes and fought for them daily. Not only did they fight over the prostitutes, but they would then beat them severely if they caught them with another man, not caring if the women died.

One day Fred watched a prostitute primp in front of a mirror at two o'clock and she was dead at five o'clock.

Fred approached the man who beat her to death and asked, "Why did you kill her?"

"I wanted to be with her, but she was primping for another man and ignored me," he stated.

This made Fred angry and he told Mr. Coultard that he would not watch the prostitutes be beaten any longer. "I will protect them from now on."

Mr. Coultard told him not to protect them. He said, "Your job is to keep the men from fighting."

"If the women are not beaten, they will keep the men happy and the men will not fight," Fred replied.

"You can protect them, but if it interferes with your job to keep the men from fighting, you will have to stop."

The prostitutes were thankful that Fred worked at Coultard's and told their friends they felt safe with him there. More and more women began asking for prostitute jobs at Coultard's. More prostitutes for the men meant fewer fights.

Patrick was never far from Coultard's Brewery, and would greet Fred each time he threw men from the brewery for fighting. On one occasion Fred asked Patrick why the men weren't arrested for killing the women.

Patrick hesitated and then answered, "There are no laws against it and no jails in which to put the men. The prostitutes have no families and no one cares what happens to them. My position is to patrol the streets."

"Why do you stay in this horrid place?" Fred asked.

"I am searching for information on the disappearance of my wife and daughter. They disappeared one day while I worked. I have not seen them since. I suspect the gangs abducted them and have either murdered them or are holding them as slaves. I pray someday I will find them alive."

Fred was disgusted with his job and all that happened in that place. He wanted to leave, but it was difficult to save dollars due to the high rent at the New Mission House.

Fred had just stopped a fight when Mr. Coultard approached him to tell him how pleased he was with his performance. He said, "Business has improved since you have been working for me. I am going to raise your wages five cents a week."

Fred stared at him and said, "I have noticed a shed behind the brewery. I would like to live there without paying rent instead of receiving a pay raise."

Mr. Coultard agreed and told him he would furnish a cot and a blanket. Fred retrieved his trunk from the New Mission House and moved into the shed. He swept the floor, slid the trunk under the cot, and used ten cents to purchase a lamp and oil. He found unused matches on the brewery floor and put them in his trunk to keep them dry. Fred lifted a loose board, dug a hole in the dirt large enough for his pouch of dollars, then covered it with dirt, and replaced the floor board. He didn't trust anyone. He worked too hard for his money to have it stolen.

Many women heard of the man who protected the prostitutes at Coultard's Brewery and came to apply for jobs. One day, as the sun was setting, Fred noticed a woman enter the brewery. When he heard her speak, he knew her voice seemed familiar. As she spoke with Mr. Coultard the lantern shone on her face. Fred was sure that he knew her and followed her into the street.

"Are you the woman who sat with me on the ship to learn English?" he asked.

She smiled and nodded.

"Why are you here?"

"I applied for a job as a prostitute. It is not what I want, but my sister and I have not been able to find work. We were not able to pay the rent and we have been living on the street. I heard of the man who protects the prostitutes at Coultard's Brewery and decided a job here was my only choice. I did not know the man was you. I will never be able to leave this place if I don't work. Mr. Coultard hired me and I will start tonight."

Fred was shaken by the thought of this woman working as a prostitute, but he knew, like him, she needed this job and would do whatever she could to earn money to leave this place.

"My name is Jane Tumbler and I am happy to see you again."

"I am Frederick Wilhelm Feldman and I will protect you the best that I can."

Each time a new woman started at the brewery the men would fight over her. Fred knew he would be busy tonight. It wasn't long before the two troublemakers were fighting over Jane. They swore at Fred and called him names, but Fred stood up to them until they finally left. Jane soon became popular with the men and they all began watching over her.

Fred and Jane spoke whenever they had the chance. He told her that he had a wife and daughter in Prussia and said he looked forward to them making the trip to America to join him. He did not say that he felt he would never see them again.

At night Fred lay in his cot thinking of Jane and struggling with the thoughts he had of her. He wanted to take her to his cot, but he still loved Wilhelmine. Even though he and Wilhelmine were divorced, he felt he must be faithful to her. He began to stay away from Jane, but the thought of her lingered in his mind day after day.

Winter passed and it seemed as though he had saved a good amount of dollars in his pouch. He would soon leave this godforsaken city of corruption.

Murder, rape, and violence became more and more prevalent. Gangs known as the Roach Guards, Dead Rabbits, and Bowery Boys dominated New York and Manhattan. Hundreds of people were killed each night. One dark and dreary night, after closing Coultard's, Fred heard shots and a rumble louder than any he had ever heard. He walked to the street, where he saw the gangs rioting. Five policemen and a woman lay dead on the street. Suddenly Fred was attacked from behind. He had no defense against so many gang members.

He heard a gang member yell, "This is that bastard that protects the whores, kill him!" They began beating him until they thought he was dead.

Days later he woke with Jane sitting beside him. He was cut and beaten so badly that it was almost impossible to recognize him. Blood still covered his body. He tried to lift his arm, but he could not. Hysteria overtook him and Jane tried to calm him.

She told him, "The gangs were rioting and attacked you. They nearly beat you to death. Mr. Coultard stopped the bleeding and stitched the cuts on your arm and face. I thought you would die."

Fred went in and out of consciousness for days, while Jane stayed at his side. When he finally woke, he could remember seeing the five policemen and a woman lying dead in the street.

"Was Patrick among the dead?" he asked.

Jane answered, "Yes, he had no chance against hundreds of gang members."

Tears streamed down Fred's face as Jane continued talking. "The Dead Rabbit gang and the Bowery Boys were rioting. The woman lay dead on the corner for several days. Her husband was afraid to fetch her body for fear the gangs were still in the neighborhood. He finally retrieved her body and dug a hole to bury her."

Fred spoke in a whisper, "When I am well, I will leave this place. Please come with me to find the farm that I dream of. You will not be safe here."

Jane nodded and said, "You need to heal and get your strength back; do not worry about me."

The days went by slowly. Fred was healing and became strong enough to stand for a short time. He was regaining the use of his arm and washed away the blood at the wash stand.

Mr. Coultard came to visit and told Fred he could stay as long as he needed. "I have already hired another man to keep the peace and I have instructed him to protect the prostitutes. You will still have your job as I can use you both."

Fred was comforted by Mr. Coultard's words, but he knew he would leave this place as soon as he was well.

Jane visited Fred each day to bring water, food, and to help him walk a few more steps. Fred knew they had feelings for each other and again he asked her to leave with him to find a farm.

"Fred, you told me that you have a wife and daughter in Prussia and someday they will join you here in America. How can I go with you?"

"Jane, I must tell you. My wife divorced me, if I do not return she will find another husband to support her. She is not strong enough to make the trip across the ocean. We promised we would see one another again, but I feel that it will never happen. I have tried to be faithful to her, but you are in my heart and I want to be with you. I have saved enough money to leave this place. Please come with me."

Fred had recovered and wanted to tell Mr. Coultard that he and Jane were leaving. He stepped into the brewery and found Mr. Coultard sitting at his usual table. "I would like to pay you for all you have done for me. I am leaving here and Jane is coming with me."

Mr. Coultard replied, "You do not owe me anything. You have been a good employee and friend. I hope your dream of owning a farm will come true."

The two troublemakers overheard their conversation and decided to be with Jane to get even with Fred for always throwing them out of the brewery.

That night Fred waited for Jane to come to him, but the hour was late and she had not arrived. He was impatient and could wait no more. It was a warm moonlit night and as he walked toward the brewery he saw something lying in the street. To his sorrow, he found Jane lying in a pool of blood, stabbed, and beaten to death. Fred sobbed and held her lifeless body until the sun rose.

A policeman was passing by and stopped to investigate. "Please find who murdered Jane," Fred sobbed.

"Murder occurs daily around here. There is nothing I can do." The officer walked away, shaking his head and muttering, "Just another one."

Fred thought of Patrick and knew even if he were alive, he would not be able to help.

Sorrow filled Fred's heart as he buried Jane in the pauper's cemetery. No marker would be placed on her grave. Her sister would never know what had happened to her as Fred did not know her sister's name or where to find her. Jane paid with her life to find a way to leave this miserable, diseased and crime-infested hole.

Fred made up his mind to leave Five Points and return to Castle Garden Immigrant Station. He felt there must be a way to leave this place. Fred asked a passing man how to return to Castle Garden and the man pointed toward a path. As Fred followed the path, many immigrants were walking toward Five Points. He knew their lives would be meaningless if they stayed there.

This time, when Fred arrived at Castle Garden, everything seemed clear to him. He looked at the maps on the wall and saw directions to a barge that was leaving for the city across the river.

Fred asked the barge master how much it would cost to ride to the other side.

"Free for immigrants. Where is your weight certificate?" the man asked.

Fred opened his trunk where he found the weight ticket marked "September" still inside. He handed it to the captain of the barge who questioned the stamped date of September, since it was now April. Fred shrugged and said, "That is when I arrived." The captain of the barge examined it again, handed it back to Fred and told him to go onto the barge.

A train was just pulling into the train station when the barge arrived on that side of the river. Fred remembered that he had stated he was going to Ohio and so purchased a ticket on the only train line, to a city called Cleveland, Ohio.

The train rumbled through New Jersey to Philadelphia, Pennsylvania, where it slowly turned northwest. Fred closed his eyes and thought of the insufferable trip across the ocean and how he ended up in Five Points. He thought of the corruption, murders, and gangs that he endured while there. The suffering had been unbearable, but if he had not found Coultard's Brewery, he would not have found Jane. Sorrow filled his heart as he thought of burying her in the pauper's cemetery. Now he must go on to find the farm for which he had already suffered so much.

FIVE
They Fought for Freedom

That night exhaustion overtook Fred and sleep engulfed him. When he woke the train had stopped. Soldiers who were wounded, bruised, and bandaged, wearing tattered uniforms and worn boots filled the train. Fred could see these young men had been aged by a war that had taken so many lives.

A soldier with his sword in its sheath at his side, sat beside Fred staring into the unknown.

Fred's English had improved greatly since he had listened to the schoolmaster. "I have heard about this war, but could you tell me why you were fighting?" he asked. The soldier stared at Fred, his face was thin and drawn, and his eyes empty of emotion.

"I can tell by your accent that you are new here," he said.

"Yes, I am Frederick Wilhelm Feldman. My homeland is Prussia. I left to find land to farm in America."

The young man said, "I was born in Aberdeen shire, Scotland and our family immigrated to America in fifty-two. We came here for freedom. When the war broke out my four older brothers enlisted in the Union Army and I followed them, with our father's permission. I was only sixteen. The war is called the Civil War. President Lincoln opposed slavery and several states declared their secession from the Union. They formed the Confederate States to fight against the Union for the right to own slaves. The

Confederate forces caused trouble at several Union forts, but the war began when they fired upon Fort Sumter, South Carolina in 1861.

"The war just ended April 9th of this year. I fought in many battles, too many to remember. I was standing guard at the Capitol the night President Lincoln was assassinated."

Fred was shocked, "I did not know the President was assassinated."

"Yes, he was shot by John Wilkes Booth on April 14th of this year, just five days after the war ended. I have seen so much devastation, and I don't know if my brothers are still alive. My parents live in Wisconsin. I have not heard from them, and I am anxious to return home." The soldier turned his head, stared back into the unknown, and did not speak again.

Fred stared out of the window as the train traveled through cities called Philadelphia, Harrisburg, and Pittsburgh. He saw many wounded soldiers with arms or legs missing. Some had bandages over their eyes; all wanting to go home to their families.

Fred overheard one soldier tell of entire plantations that were burned to the ground and families all killed. Some soldiers could barely speak and would never be the same again. Fred looked deeply into each man's eyes and knew they had all lived through hell.

Once again Fred thought of the tumultuous travel by ship, with death and disease all around. He thought of murder and riots at Five Points. He thought of Mr. Coultard, Patrick, Wilhelmine, Sophie, Jane, and now this war. His trip to America had been filled with turmoil and coming here had not been what he expected. Sorrow and the lack of compassion were everywhere.

When they arrived in Pittsburg, the soldier sitting beside Fred stood to leave, then turned and said, "I am changing trains to travel north to Wisconsin where I believe I will find my family.

Good luck in America, Frederick Wilhelm Feldman. I hope you find all that you want."

The soldier stepped from the train and disappeared. Fred realized he had not asked his name.

Another soldier boarded the train and sat beside Fred.

"Are you returning home from the war?" Fred asked.

"Yes, it has been a long and wretched war. I hope to never see such a thing again. Rotting bodies of men and animals were everywhere. Arms and legs stuck out of hastily dug graves. Each time I close my eyes I see the men that I had to kill to defend myself. Their faces are etched into my mind as if chiseled in stone. I watched as men were dragged to a doctor who sawed off their mangled and shattered limbs. There was little ether to sedate the men. The screaming went on and on, more died than lived. Amputated limbs were thrown into piles to rot. Our regiment moved a mile away, but the smell of human decay was bitter and carried on the wind.

"We carried no identification and began writing our names on cloth or paper and attached our hastily made label to our uniform jacket in hopes our families would hear of our demise."

The man took a letter from his pocket and said, "I found this letter on the body of a Union soldier whose wife wrote...

> My dearest Henry, if you die in this godforsaken war, I will miss you the rest of my life, but I know you will not have died in vain. If you return home I shall rejoice. I will love you always.
>
> Your loving wife, Ellen

Her address is Cleveland, Ohio. I am going there to find her and return this letter. It is the least I can do."

"I will be dismissed from the 23rd Ohio Volunteer Infantry Regiment in Cleveland, and paid for my service in the war. I hear there are many jobs there, and I will be able to start a new life."

SIX
Cleveland

Fred watched from the window as the train pulled into the Cleveland train station. He could not believe how this city was thriving, unlike the devastated cities of Pennsylvania. As he stepped from the train, the sound of hammers driving nails rang through the air. He walked toward the sound and stared up at the buildings, one towering over the other. Mansions larger than anything he had ever seen were being built. Cleveland had grown during the war as it sold rifles and uniforms to the army.

The street he walked was bustling with people. Breweries, restaurants, barber shops, garment shops, and woolen mills lined the street. Smoke from oil refineries filled the sky. Shipyards were busy building ships for use on the Great Lakes. Fred had never seen such a city.

He wandered past Cherry Street and was surprised to see a fine, white-faced bay colt, with one white hoof caught in a grate. He had worked with many horses in Prussia and knew the frightened horse would be severely injured if he wasn't set free soon. Fred took a piece of dried fruit from his trunk and held it out to the colt. Hunger had overtaken the colt and it settled down to eat the offered treat. Fred then knelt and slipped the horse's hoof from the grate. There was a pasture of horses in the distance and Fred walked in that direction as the colt followed.

Fred followed a fine, white fence. A man standing at the gate told him the colt had strayed from his premises.

"I am Frederick Wilhelm Feldman. I am looking for work. I was a farmer in Prussia and took care of many horses."

"What other work can you do?" the man asked.

Fred answered, "I will try anything you ask of me; if you are not happy, I will leave."

The man thought about the horse following Fred without a lead rope and knew Fred must have a way with horses. "I am William Lampton, and I will give you a job as a reward. You can bunk in the stable with the horses. Make a bed in the straw, wash up at the pump outside, and come to the house to eat."

It had been a long time since Fred had had such a meal. Tender beef, potatoes, and green beans filled his plate. He would sleep with a full stomach and without worry. There were no thoughts of the past months tonight as he fell to sleep the instant he lay down.

A gentle nudging woke Fred in the morning. "Well, how did you get out of your pen?" Fred asked the colt he had rescued the day before. The colt nudged and pushed Fred toward the feed bunk.

Just then Mr. Lampton stepped into the stable and began to laugh. "That colt has always been able to open his gate. I thought I had it fixed. I will show you what needs to be done each day. First carry buckets of water to the horses and feed them, turn them into the pasture and scoop the manure from their stalls."

It didn't take Fred long to settle into the routine. He worked hard and Mr. Lampton seemed happy with him. Fred enjoyed working for Mr. Lampton; he was a fair and honest man, but the dream of owning a farm still haunted Fred, and again, he saved his dollars to leave Cleveland and follow his dream.

Fred felt that he should write to Wilhelmine, but he could not tell her the truth of all that had happened or the misery he had suffered. His heart was filled with sad memories and empty of emotion. He thought by spring he would be able to save enough dollars to travel on, and find his own farm.

8-12-1865

42 Cherry Street

Cleveland, Ohio

My Dearest Wilhelmine and Sophie,

The trip to America was long, but I arrived at the port of Baltimore, September 12, 1864. It was difficult to understand where I should go as I could not read the papers given to me. I found my way to Castle Garden Immigrant Station on an island called Manhattan and followed other immigrants to a place named Five Points, where Mr. Coultard hired me to work for him. I was able to live in a shed on Mr. Coultard's property and save dollars to purchase land, but I do not know how many dollars I will need to purchase land.

I rode the train to Cleveland, Ohio and on the way I sat beside soldiers who told me a war, called the Civil War, had just ended, and President Lincoln had been assassinated just five days after the war ended.

Cleveland, Ohio is most pleasant with tall buildings and mansions so wonderful it is impossible to describe them.

Upon walking by Cherry Street in Cleveland, I found a young bay colt whose foot was caught in a grate, but I was able to free him.

I saw a pasture in the distance; the colt followed me to that farm. Mr. Lampton owned the colt and farm and has given me a job. It is a good job and I am able to save a few dollars.

I will stay here until spring and then travel on. Please write as soon as you receive this letter and tell me how you and Sophie are doing. I pray we will see each other again.

With all my love, Frederick

Fred folded two of his precious dollars and tucked them inside the envelope. Wilhelmine would be able to exchange them for silver coins. It was difficult for him to part with the dollars, but he knew Wilhelmine needed them far more than he did. Fred's thoughts were filled with dreams of Wilhelmine and Sophie. He thought of the love he had for Wilhelmine, and the love they made, especially the last time before he left for America. They had spoken of the possibility of never seeing each other again, and had made love into the dawn as their tears intermingled. He would love Wilhelmine and Sophie, forever, but he still had feelings and memories of Jane. He thought how his feelings for Jane were strong, and how he stayed away from her to be faithful to Wilhelmine. He remembered the desire he had for Jane as he waited for her to come to his cot the night he found her lifeless body lying on the street. He loved them both, each in a different way and he would think of them forever.

Cold winds blew across the lake, freezing the ground and all that grew in it. Winter was upon Cleveland. The stable was cold and almost unbearable. At night Fred snuggled into the straw and prayed this would be his last winter in Cleveland. He worked hard during the day to stay warm, and was thankful that he was able to save a few dollars for a farm of his own.

One day a black man, who introduced himself as George Irving, came to Mr. Lampton's farm and asked for work. George said that he had been a slave before the war, but now he carried his papers of freedom. The man looked tired, his clothes were worn and ragged, and his feet were bare. Mr. Lampton may have felt sympathy for him or possibly he thought Fred needed help, none-the-less, he hired him.

George told them, "I left the South after men in robes come to our cabin. They broke in the door and drug my wife and child to the nearest tree and hung'em. I begged'em to hang me and let my family go, but they didn't listen. Our master had given us our freedom papers, but these men said all black men should be slaves. They made me watch my wife and child take their last breaths. They let my wife down and put the rope around my neck. Just then lawmen came along and the men in robes ran into the trees. The officers told me to go far north, where I would find work and be safe from those men."

A tear rolled down George's face as he went on to say, "There is a lot of bad stuff going on in the South since the war. Men from the North, carrying big bags, are robbing southerners, stealing land, and getting into politics. I heard 'em called 'Carpetbaggers.' Bushwhackers are killing, robbing banks and stagecoaches, scalping the dead and tying the scalps to their saddles. These men are up to no good. It was difficult coming here. I hid many times while men in robes and bushwhackers passed by me."

Fred and Mr. Lampton were stunned to hear of the events that were taking place around them. Everything seemed peaceful in Cleveland.

Mr. Lampton told Fred to show George the stable and help him make a bed in the straw. Fred took George inside, pulled his trunk from under the straw, and opened it. "It is too cold for you to wear those ragged pants and have nothing on your feet. I carried these pants and boots from Prussia and have not needed them. I want you to have them. My trunk will be lighter with them gone."

"Are you leaving?" George asked.

"I will leave as soon as I hear from my wife in Prussia. I am hoping to hear from her by spring." Fred replied.

The winter was long and cold with more snow than Fred and George had ever seen. They stayed busy moving the snow and doing the chores. The bay colt was always near Fred, wherever he went, and continued to wake him each morning. The straw beds kept the men warm at night, and the generous meals that Mrs. Lampton prepared helped warm them throughout the day.

SEVEN
Moving on

The warm spring sun thawed the earth and melted the icicles that hung from the stable. Fred prayed that he would receive a letter from Wilhelmine soon. He was anxious to leave and find his own farm, somewhere, in America.

Spring came and went. Summer passed as the sun bore down upon the earth with a fury. Crops were taken from the fields and Fred knew he would have to spend another winter hoping to hear from Wilhelmine. Another difficult winter passed. Fred felt trapped in this city and thought he would never hear from Wilhelmine. As he worked, he decided to tell Mr. Lampton that he was leaving.

Just then Mr. Lampton stepped into the stable and asked Fred to go to town for supplies and the mail. "Here is the list of supplies that I need. Tell Mr. Aldred that I will be there to pay my bill in two weeks."

Fred looked at Mr. Lampton and asked, "What year is this?"

"It is March 15, 1867. Why do you ask?"

"Three years have passed since I left my homeland of Prussia for America. I wished to have my own farm by now, but I am beginning to believe it will never happen."

"Are you unhappy here?"

"No, you have been very kind and it is good working for you. I left my family behind to fulfill my dream, and it is time to move on." Fred hitched the horse to the wagon and left for town.

Stepping into the general store, Fred handed the list to Mr. Aldred and told him that Mr. Lampton would be here in two weeks to pay him. Mr. Aldred was a sober man and had few words to say. He nodded and began gathering the items on the list. The items were sugar, flour, candles, salted pork, beans, coffee, crackers, and many more essentials.

Fred stepped outside to wait and noticed a man nailing a poster to the building. He was curious and walked up to the man. "What does this poster mean?" he asked

The man answered, "I have just returned from the state of Iowa. This is a decree from that state proclaiming that there is land to homestead. If you live on it for five years, the land will be yours."

Fred could hardly believe what he was hearing. "Where is Iowa?" he asked.

"The train will take you to Rock Island. It is a city located along the Mississippi River on the eastern edge of Iowa. The northwestern part of Iowa has very few settlers. You would have a better chance to homestead there. The southern part of the state is almost all homesteaded. From Rock Island you can take the train to Fort Dodge where you will be able to purchase supplies. The Little Sioux River lays northwest of Fort Dodge. Trees grow along the banks of the river, and the soil is black and rich. Few trees grow on the prairie. You will need them to build a cabin."

Fred watched the man leave, and pulled down the poster that told of Iowa. "I will find Iowa as soon as I hear from Wilhelmine," he muttered to himself.

The supplies were loaded into the wagon, and he began to leave when he realized, in his excitement, he had forgotten to pick up the mail. He pulled the horse to a stop and walked to the post office.

"Sir," Fred asked, "do you have mail for Mr. William Lampton?"

The postmaster reached into a small box and brought out a few letters. "Here is a letter for Frederick Wilhelm Feldman. Is there a man of that name at Mr. Lampton's address?"

Fred's heart beat so hard he could barely speak. "Yes, I am Frederick Wilhelm Feldman and I am expecting a letter."

He hurried to the wagon and stared at the letter from Wilhelmine Feldman. Her handwriting was dainty and precise. Three years had passed since he had held her soft and fragile body and smelled her scent of sweet lavender. He remembered how her long, blond hair fell over her shoulders as she took it from the twist on top of her head.

He would read the letter tonight when supplies were delivered, and the chores done for the day. Fred tucked the letter into his smock, along with the poster, and slapped the reigns against the horse.

His only thoughts were of the letter as he unloaded the supplies, finished his chores, and ate the evening meal. He washed at the pump and buried himself in his bed of straw. His hands shook as he slowly opened the only words he had had from home for these three years. He was anxious to read the letter, but afraid of what she might say. Fred noticed the letter was dated November 18, 1866. He knew the ship would not cross the ocean in winter, and that explained why it had taken so long for Wilhelmine's letter to arrive.

George stepped into the stable and watched as Fred opened the letter. He stepped back into the cool spring night, leaving Fred to read his letter alone.

> November 18, 1866
>
> Dear beloved Frederick,
>
> I was happier than I can say when I received your letter. The thought of you reaching

America alive brought tears to my eyes... so many I could barely read the words that you wrote.

Otto von Bismarck has taken us to war. Prussia deliberately challenged Austria for the leadership of the German Confederation. They fought for the leadership of Schleswig and Holstein. After victory over Austria, Prussia organized the North German Confederation. Otto von Bismarck made himself the North German "Bundeskangler." (Head Executive)

Sophie is three years old. Each time she has a birthday I am reminded again how long it has been since you left for America. She walks and talks and is a happy child. I fear as she grows older her happiness will disappear.

I am struggling with the words to tell you of our fate since you left. Father was forced to close his business due to the war. He was distraught and I am afraid his financial troubles were his undoing. August Kolbus held the mortgage on his house and business, and as you know, August is not lenient with those who owe him money. Father sold all that he could to pay August, but it was not enough.

August came late one night and demanded to be paid in full, but Father could do no more. We heard them arguing, but we did not rise from our beds ... if only we had, it might have been different. Sometime after August left, Father went to the shed and hung himself.

Mother and I found him the next morning. We dug a hole by the shed and buried Father after praying over him. We did not have money to hire the undertaker. My heart is filled with sorrow that we could not give him a proper burial, and there is no marker to tell that he lived. I pray someday we will all be together again.

August Kolbus came as we buried Father and demanded that we leave the house . . . giving us two days. That afternoon I went to August and asked where he thought we should go? He was evil and sneered as he told me that he did not care where we went. I said, "My mother is old, and I have a small daughter. We need a place to live, and we have no money." He stared into my eyes for a long time, than leaned back in his chair.

"You can live with me," he said. "I will be your guardian, and you will cook and clean for me. Bring your clothes and leave the rest, you won't need anything else."

We have lived with August for several months. Mother cooks and I clean. Sophie is still happy and doesn't mind being here. August is an evil man, but if we do everything he asks of us there is no problem. There doesn't seem to be any way out of this as we have no place else to go, and we have no silver. At least we are safe here.

On Wednesday August will send me to the market, at which time I will mail this letter and exchange the American dollars you sent for silver. I will tuck the silver away for a time when it is needed. Thank you for your generosity.

I think of you always, and at night I remember the love we made our last time together and how you held me so close. I will love you forever.

Your beloved, Wilhelmine and Sophie"

Fred was filled with sorrow. He did not think his family would end up as servants to August Kolbus. If only they would have traveled to America with him.

EIGHT
Declaration of Intent

The sun glistened against the early morning dew as Fred approached Mr. Lampton.

"I have received a letter from Wilhelmine and have this poster that hung on a building when I went to town for supplies yesterday. It says there is land to homestead in Iowa. The land will belong to me if I live on a claim for five years and plant trees, or pay one dollar and twenty five cents an acre. I will leave tomorrow to find land in Iowa."

Mr. Lampton was happy to hear that Fred might find land to own. "I will miss you, but I know that you need to go. I have heard of the Homestead Act. You must have proof that you have lived in America for two years, and file a Declaration of Intent to homestead land. When you find land, you will need to find a land office and file homestead papers which state you are living on the land."

Fred took his passage papers from his trunk and showed them to Mr. Lampton.

"I am sure that is all you need, but I will go to the county court with you and testify that you have lived with me for two years, if necessary."

The trip to the county court seemed farther than it was. Fred was anxious to leave for Iowa and felt this was an inconvenience, but he knew he had to abide by the law. His ship passage papers were all that he needed to file a Declaration of Intent. The man, who filled out the paper work, was a pleasant man and said, "You will have to wait three years to become a citizen."

Fred was content that he held the papers he needed to homestead land.

He asked the man, "If I find land in northwest Iowa where would I find a land office to file homestead papers?"

The clerk was surprised that Fred knew he would have to file homestead papers. "There is a land office in Sioux City, Iowa. Sioux City lies along the Missouri River, which is on the western border of Iowa." He went on to say, "Northwest Iowa has been declared a useless slough, which is discouraging most homesteaders from traveling there, but I have heard a few good stories about that part of the state.

Travel to Fort Dodge, Iowa where you will be able to purchase supplies. When you leave Fort Dodge, travel northwest to find the river called the Little Sioux." The man hesitated, then continued telling his story. "The Little Sioux River winds through northwest Iowa. The river has trees along its banks to build a cabin, and there are fur-bearing animals to trap. I understand the soil is rich and black. They tell me that many years ago the Santee Sioux Indians roamed northwest Iowa, but I understand they are gone now.

Still, few immigrants have traveled to that part of Iowa."

Fred believed that he would find land as this was the second man to tell him about the Little Sioux River with trees along its bank and northwest Iowa's rich soil.

He thanked the man for the information and turned to Mr. Lampton, "I will leave in the morning."

He would miss Mr. Lampton, George, and the bay colt he called Freedom. Fred believed that Freedom had led him to Cherry Street, where he could follow his path to citizenship and land to homestead.

Fred's sleep was restless knowing he would leave Cleveland in the morning. Once again, he dreamed of his life with Wilhelmine and Sophie; his life at Five Points with Mr. Coultard, Patrick, and Jane, and his life here with Mr. Lampton, George, and Freedom. Each time he had left those he loved behind to find the land he so craved.

Freedom nuzzled Fred to wake him as he had done each morning since Fred had moved into the stable. Fred stood, looked into Freedom's eyes and said, "I will leave today and never return. I believe you led me here so I would find my way to Iowa." Tears ran down Fred's face as the colt nuzzled against him; he seemed to know he would never see Fred again. Fred would miss the colt that led him to Mr. Lampton's farm, woke him each morning, and followed him wherever he went. He was a gentle colt who wanted freedom as much as Fred wanted it.

George and Mr. Lampton shook Fred's rough and calloused hand, wishing him a good journey. Fred threw his trunk over his shoulder and walked down the road past the white fence he had followed to arrive at Mr. Lampton's farm. Freedom followed along snorting and trotting to keep up. Fred stopped one last time, patted Freedom and said, "I will always remember you." Fred's heart was heavy, but also full of anticipation and excitement as he left for yet another new life.

NINE
Iowa

Fred stepped up to the ticket window at the Cleveland train depot and asked to purchase a ticket to Fort Dodge. The ticket agent peered over his glasses. "You will have to purchase a ticket to Rock Island, cross the Mississippi River on a ferry, and then purchase a ticket for the train to Fort Dodge."

After purchasing a ticket to Rock Island, Fred boarded the train and settled into a seat. He watched the mansions, ship yards, and factories of Cleveland disappear as the train rumbled toward Iowa and the Mississippi River.

When Fred arrived in Rock Island he could see that Rock Island was still growing and not as large as Cleveland, but he was amazed by the size of the Mississippi River and couldn't take his eyes off the wide and fast moving river. He had never seen such a river.

It was dusk, and the ferry did not cross the river at night. Opening his trunk, Fred pushed his hand inside where he felt the handle of his precious knife. Once again, he was comforted to know the knife was still there. Little jerky and dried fruit remained. Fred closed the trunk and did not eat.

Fred lay on the ground gazing at the stars and listening to steamboats blow their horns as they made their way, carrying supplies, to the growing cities along the river's banks. As so many nights before, he thought of Wilhelmine, Sophie, and Jane.

Thoughts of the places he had been, the friends he had made, and Freedom, the bay colt, filled his mind until he slept.

The next morning Fred crossed the river on the ferry, and found the train depot to purchase a ticket to Fort Dodge.

The depot agent was a dull man and hardly looked up when Fred asked to purchase a ticket to Fort Dodge. "The tracks are not complete to Fort Dodge; you will have to purchase a ticket to Cedar Falls," he stated in a dry, monotone voice.

"Where is Cedar Falls?" Fred asked.

"East of Fort Dodge," was the reply.

A ticket to Cedar Falls was purchased, and Fred wondered if there would be enough money to buy oxen and supplies. He boarded the train and watched as the landscape changed from hills and trees to flat land and prairie grass.

When he arrived in Cedar Falls, Fred asked a man for directions to the livery. The gentleman pointed to an unkempt building down the street. It was a dimly lit livery that smelled of animal dung. A few underfed horses were eating a handful of oats.

"Would you have a yoke of oxen that I could purchase?" Fred asked the smithy.

The man continued hammering a horse shoe as he nodded to a pair of big, red oxen in a small pen. "That yoke of oxen will cost sixty dollars. I will sell you a harness for two dollars and a wagon for six dollars."

"I will take them all if you help me harness them," Fred replied.

The smithy put down the hammer and began harnessing the oxen. They seemed a bit wild, and Fred glanced around to see if there could be another pair, but these were the only oxen in the stable. Fred held out his dollars and the smithy counted the amount he needed. To Fred's amazement, he still had money for supplies. He drove the oxen to the general store where he bought salt, sugar, flour, coffee, bacon, tobacco, soap, a coffee pot, grinder, kettle, frying pan, water pail, hand ax, a length of rope, twine, six chickens in a cage, a pig, feed for the animals, whiplash, breaking plow, wheat seed, a gun, powder, and powder horn. To Fred's surprise a small amount of money still remained.

Fred felt he had bought his oxen for a fair price, but when he tried to steer them out of Cedar Falls he discovered they were wild in their disposition. It was difficult to steer them in any direction, but the one they wanted to go. The head strong, big, red oxen did not heed Fred's pull on the reigns. They turned the opposite direction that Fred steered them, ran over a hitching post, and barely missed hitting people. When they finally stopped, he tied the newly purchased rope around each ox's horns. Holding the other end of the rope, he could pull the oxen's heads sideways to turn them, go backwards, or stop.

The sun was high overhead when he turned his oxen northwest. He was filled with the hope of finding the Little Sioux River and land to homestead. It was dark when he stopped for the night.

Tired and weary, he lay on the ground under his wagon and wondered what lay ahead. Would he find the Little Sioux River? Was the Little Sioux as wide and treacherous as the Mississippi River? If it was as wide and deep, how would he cross it? Were the stories of the rich, black soil true? Would there be other settlers, and were the Indians truly gone? He drifted off to sleep with thoughts and questions he never had before.

Dawn was breaking when the oxen began to stir. Fred built a fire using dried dung and prairie grass. Matches from the floor of Coultard's Brewery were still tucked away in his trunk, dry enough to strike and light a fire. He was hungry and a slice of bacon with coffee would start his day. As he sliced bacon from the slab, he heard a wagon approaching.

"Hello," a man called. "We saw the smoke from your fire as we crossed the prairie."

Fred invited the family to step down and enjoy bacon and coffee, but they declined. "Where are you traveling to so early in the morning?" he asked.

"Our baby is sick. We traveled all night to return to Cedar Falls to find a doctor," the man replied. "We have lost two children to diphtheria and will lose this one if we do not find a doctor. We must save him. He is all we have left. We have lived through two years of hot summers, cold winters, prairie fires, and land with little fresh water, sickness, and the death of our children."

"I am sorry to hear of your sorrow," Fred told them. As they began to leave Fred asked, "Were you living near the Little Sioux River?"

"I have never heard of that river. We lived on a useless slough with little land to farm. We should have left long ago."

This was the second man to tell Fred that northwest Iowa was nothing but a useless slough. However, he had also been told twice that the land in northwest Iowa was rich and fertile. He considered turning back, but he had come too far to go back. He ate his bacon, drank the coffee, hitched his oxen to the wagon, and drove them northwest. A few swampy areas provided the only water that he found.

He enjoyed the warm and pleasant spring days as he traveled toward the unknown. His big, red oxen still had a mind of their own and after a few days they turned due west. Fred gave them their head. He thought they might find the river he was so determined to find.

A sod house sat in the distance, but it looked deserted. He reasoned that it could have belonged to the family who was headed to Cedar Falls to find a doctor for their child, and he continued on.

Fred drove day after day, his mind filled with thoughts of all he had gone through. He continued to wonder if there were settlers in northwest Iowa, if Indians still roamed the land, and what might lie ahead?

TEN
Land and Neighbors

Fred traveled on, and each day passed . . . one like the other . . . until he saw hills in the distance. The oxen lifted their heads, sniffed the air, and picked up their pace. Fred felt certain they could smell water. It was midday when he heard the sound of water rushing over rocks. He pulled the oxen to a halt as he gazed over a lush and green valley. A river, not as wide or deep or swift as the Mississippi River, but lined with trees, wound its way through the land. Everything he dreamed of was here.

Prairie flowers blooming and birds singing filled Fred with a sense of peacefulness he had not felt in a long time. He crossed the river to a flat piece of land and stepped down from his wagon. Taking his spade from the wagon he cleared a patch of sod and dug deep into the earth. He brought up rich, black soil, and felt he had found northwest Iowa and the Little Sioux River. The land was rough. Rocks and prairie grass would need to be cleared; nonetheless, this would be his home.

He could tell it was still early spring and if he hurried he would be able to plant his first crop. The next day he began clearing rocks and cutting prairie grass from the area to be plowed and planted. He would use the rocks for his chimney and fireplace. Weeks passed before the land was ready for the breaking plow. Prairie grass roots grew deep and were difficult to plow. Swinging his whiplash over the oxen's backs, he urged them on. The big, red oxen pulled with all their strength, and little by little, they plowed furrows in a straight line, smooth and even. Fred ran the rich, black soil through his fingers and smelled the mellow earth, then planted his precious seed in the furrows. Now all he needed was rain.

With the planting done Fred began to build a sod house. He would save the trees for firewood, poles to sell, and a stable.

He chose a flat area and began the tedious job of cutting sod bricks with his spade. Pushing the spade deep into the roots would insure that they would grow and bind the bricks together. Fred carefully cut each brick in three foot lengths, twelve inches wide and four inches thick. He placed the rows alternately, lengthwise and crosswise.

Fred did not know how long he had been here or what the date was. Spring flooding had subsided and the water was low in the river. The days were hot and becoming shorter. He worked hard to finish his soddy and paid little attention to his surroundings. One day he was surprised to see smoke rising from the top of the hill across the river. The next day he hitched his big, red oxen to the wagon and traveled to meet his neighbors.

The big, red oxen crossed the river with ease and headed across the flat land to a steep hill. The oxen were strong and pulled hard to reach the top. A cabin with smoke billowing from the chimney sat overlooking the valley where a creek joined the river.

A swarthy, pleasant man of six feet, hair and full beard of light color, and clear blue eyes opened the door. The man introduced himself as Hannibal Waterman, his wife as Hannah, and their children.

By contrast, Fred was an unusual sight at five foot eight inches tall, weighing about one hundred and fifty pounds, and wearing a dark beard. His trousers were thrust into his boot tops. He wore a smock made of cotton grain sacks sewed together with heavy twine. The smock, after the style worn by field laborers in Prussia, came below his waist line, outside his trousers. Hannibal had never seen anyone dressed in such a manner.

Fred introduced himself, "I am Frederick Wilhelm Feldman. I have emigrated from Prussia and I am homesteading land in the valley across the river. I saw your smoke and came to visit."

Hannibal thought a moment and replied, "I will not be able to remember such a long and difficult name. Since you are from Prussia, I will call you "Dutch Fred."

Fred laughed and gladly accepted the appellation. "Are there other people living in the area?" he then asked.

Hannibal answered, "There are several families living in the village of Peterson, east of here. It is necessary to cross the river again to travel there."

"How long have you lived here? Are there Indians here?"

"We came here in July of 1856. The Indians lived here when we arrived. They came often for food, but they are gone and I'm sure they will not return."

"What year is this?" Fred asked.

"It is 1867." Hannibal replied.

Fred could hardly believe the Waterman's had lived here over ten years.

"Come in; we will visit as we eat."

The smell of freshly baked bread filled the hot, but cozy cabin. An open Bible lay on the table. Hannah sliced the warm bread, set gooseberry jam and butter, whipped that morning after milking the cow, on the table and poured the coffee. Hannibal read a verse from the Bible and thanked God for food and the company of a neighbor.

"Your bread, butter, and jam are most delicious," Fred told Hannah. "I have not tasted such a treat in a long time."

When they finished eating Hannah cleared the table, while Hannibal told Fred of coming to northwest Iowa. "I was born in

New York. When I heard of the rich soil and the Little Sioux River with trees along its banks, I could think of nothing else. I traveled to Bremer County, Iowa, where I met my wife, Hannah. That is where we married, and our first child, Emily, was born."

"We both wanted to travel to northwest Iowa and find land to own. Each day we traveled through prairie grass so tall that it towered over us. The hot July sun scorched our skin and the wind blew dust into our wagon. Hannah covered the trunk containing our food with a quilt, but the dust still sifted in."

The Kirchner cabin remains today, near the city of Peterson, Iowa.

"Sometimes I would doze as the oxen plodded on. One day, when I opened my eyes, I saw people building a cabin in the distance. The settlers introduced themselves as Christian and Magdalena Kirchner and family. They live east of here near the city of Peterson. Ambrose Meade, the James Bicknell family, and the Taylor family are other settlers that live near Peterson.

"Christian told us to drive to the top of the hill and we would find land to own. He said the Sioux Indians came to beg for food, but they were peaceful. We found this place, where the creek joins the river. It was July 11, 1856, and too late to plant wheat or a garden. We gathered berries and nuts, caught fish to preserve with salt for the winter, and built this cabin. Thousands of prairie chickens roamed here, but they were almost impossible to catch. I devised a trap, but the prairie chickens were cunning and I only captured a few. Hannah finally told me to stop trapping them. She said they had little meat on their bones and weren't worth the effort to catch."

"Our first winter was hard. We had few supplies and the Indians came often wanting food. Hank Meyer, a one armed man who worked for me, traveled to Fort Dodge for supplies, but he was unable to purchase all that we needed. Hannah used the last of our flour to make bread pudding for our Christmas dinner. After Christmas Hank left to find more supplies, but he became snowbound at a stranger's cabin and could not return until spring. The Sioux continued to come throughout the winter. Their chief was old and his face was scarred from smallpox. His band called him "Inkpadutah." We had little food to give them and we only ate one meal a day ourselves. We hid our small amount of supplies in a cellar under the cabin. Thankfully, the Sioux did not realize there could be such a thing. To our relief the band left, but returned in a few weeks. We heard later that settlers took the band's few guns away from them at Smithland where they had hoped to hunt for elk. They became angry, stole guns at Correctionville, and returned to our cabin wearing war paint. They plundered our cabin and took whatever they wanted. A squaw took Hannah's shawl from her shoulders, but Hannah did not move from her chair. Our kitten was hiding under her apron and Emily sat on her lap. None of them moved or I am afraid the Sioux would have slaughtered all of us. The band killed our cow, ate what they wanted, and left the rest lying by the cabin.

"Still hungry and angry, they went to the Kirchner cabin where they killed an ox and demanded that Magdalena cook the meat. Christian told me later that the band began eating the meat before it was thoroughly cooked. Blood ran down their chins and arms, mixing with the war paint, covering the table and floor. It must have been a gruesome sight. Christian said the band then went to the Meade cabin, where the Taylors had gone for safety. The Sioux took Mrs. Taylor and Mrs. Meade to their teepees, releasing them after two nights. Who knows what those poor women endured. We heard sometime later that the band went to Spirit Lake country and massacred many settlers. They took a young girl, Abby Gardner, and three women captive. Two of the women were killed trying to escape. The girl and other woman were sold back to the white people sometime later.

"Three years had passed since the Sioux left. We lived in peace in this quiet and serene valley until seven men approached our cabin. The men introduced themselves as officers of Woodbury County. I told them we lived in Clay County, but they replied that Clay County was east of here and this part of Woodbury County would soon become O'Brien County. The men demanded that we hold an election, and I was elected treasurer. I now realize they needed me to make the election legal as I was the only citizen of the new county. The men told me they would name the creek and township Waterman. I believe it was to insure I would vote with them. They were schemers and held meetings without me. They turned in bills to the new county of O'Brien for bridges that were never built, roads that were never made, and supplies that were never purchased, putting the new county thousands of dollars in debt. They built a court house on my land and jumped my claim. They demanded that I resign as treasurer, and then they would sell my land back to me for one $100.00. I told them to move that court house from my land and I would resign. A man named Tiffey purchased a tract of land and the court house was moved onto his land. The first town, named O'Brien, and county government were established there in 1860."

Fred was curious, and asked, "Did the Sioux ever return?"

Hannibal answered, "They were not seen again until after the Civil War began in 1861. The government built a fort in Peterson in 1862. When the Sioux returned, the soldiers chased them far into the Dakotas. It has been reported that the band fled into Canada where Inkpadutah died."

After the Civil War, part of Fort Peterson was moved to a farm west of Peterson until several years ago when it was moved back to its original location and restored.

After hearing Hannibal's story, Fred spoke in his native accent. "All hold office but me, and I am de peoples." Fred shook his smock, laughed and said, "Des be a poor man mit clothes, but Dutch Fred be under here just like udder mans."

Fred told Hannibal, "I left Prussia to escape the emperor's wrath and war. I was thirty-seven and did not want to fight in war. The Emperor would have forced me to join the army regardless of my age." Fred was a private man and did not mention his wife and daughter, or his travels to this place.

Hannibal pointed southeast, "The town of O'Brien is just over that hill. Squire Sage has a general store there, and you will be able to purchase supplies. He will write them down until your crop is harvested."

This sign states that the town of O'Brien had been located on this land.

As Fred headed toward the town of O'Brien, he pondered all that Hannibal had told him. He felt pleasure in the fact that the Indians were gone and a town was near his homestead.

He turned the big, red oxen toward smoke billowing in the distance. When he reached the smoke, he saw men making bricks of clay and firing them in the ravine. Fred stopped to watch and asked a man how the bricks would be used.

"We are making bricks to build a school house in the town. Mrs. Waterman holds class in her home, but it will be better to have a school building."

When he drove into the town, he saw the court house, a few houses, and H.A. Sage's General Store. He pulled his oxen to a stop in front of the general store. One window facing the south let in a small amount of light and a lantern hung over the counter where a man stood waiting for a paltry number of customers. The smell of freshly cut wood lingered in the air. A floor board creaked as Fred stepped inside.

Fred introduced himself as Dutch Fred and H.A. Sage introduced himself as Squire Sage.

"What can I do for you?" Sage asked.

"I would like coffee, jerky, salt, and tobacco. I do not have money, but if you would write the items down, I will pay when I harvest my crop. I will make money by cutting rails for fences and firewood to sell."

"Where is your homestead located," Sage inquired.

"My homestead is west of here and across the river."

Squire Sage wrote the items in a book and turned to take a scythe down from the wall. "You will need this to harvest your wheat. Make sure you keep it sharp. You can sell your wheat in Peterson at the Kirchner Mill. Good luck with your harvest and return when you need supplies."

The wheat grew tall and turned from a lush green to a golden hue. Each day Fred checked the wheat heads until the seed was ready to be harvested. When it was ready, he swung the scythe, cutting his crop with ease. He tied the wheat into bundles and stood them on end until they were dry. When they dried, he beat the stalks on the edge of the pail as the seeds fell inside. A gentle breeze blew the chaff away, leaving straw to bed down the animals and pails full of seed. Fred traveled to Peterson where he sold the wheat at the Kirchner Mill. The town of O'Brien lay between Fred's homestead and Peterson. When Fred returned from Peterson, he stopped to pay his debt at Squire Sage's General Store, and bought more supplies for the winter ahead, using most of his dollars.

ELEVEN
A New Fangled Machine

The big, red oxen were continually wandering off. Fred stacked rocks around an area to keep them from wandering away. When he ran out of rocks, he dug dirt ridges, but the rocks and ridges did not keep the oxen in. He cut down trees and made rails and stakes to build a fence, which kept them in . . . most of the time. After building a fence he cut poles to build a stable. He set the poles straight and erect in holes that he dug with his spade. He lined the roof with poles, and when he finished he covered them with a thick layer of prairie grass (in a great amount) to keep the stable dry in summer and warm in winter. He did not own a saw, but he was handy with his ax, which he sharpened on his grindstone.

Building a homestead was a continuous work of labor. Now that his soddy and stable were finished, he began cutting trees for poles and firewood to sell throughout winter.

It was a bitter winter and existence was a grim struggle. The river was frozen so deep it was almost impossible to cut deep enough into the ice to reach water. The big, red oxen knocked down the fence and wandered away looking for water. Fred needed his oxen and feared they would get lost and die. Each day he rounded up the oxen and worked to fix fence and cut ice.

When he wasn't fixing fence or cutting ice, he was building furniture. He made a bed frame from the small trees that he cut along the river. He sewed the cloth wheat sacks together, stuffing them with dried prairie grass that he had cut when the weather was warm . . . making a comfortable mattress. After building a bed, he made a table and chairs and a stand to hold the water pail, with a shelf for tallow, soap, and other supplies.

One day as he was cutting ice, two men crossed the river and introduced themselves as Wm. H. Baker and his nephew Ed. Fred invited them in to drink coffee and warm themselves by the fire.

The men had heard of the river in northwest Iowa with trees along its banks and fur-bearing animals to trap. They told Fred they came to make their fortune trapping. Wm. and Ed stopped often to visit and drink coffee. Each time they stopped they had many furs which would be sold to the fur buyer in Cherokee.

It would soon be spring, and Fred's supplies were low. He would have to cross the river before the spring flooding. He hitched his big, red oxen to the wagon and crossed on the still frozen river.

Fred's dollars were gone after he paid Squire Sage for last year's wheat and supplies, but he was sure Sage would write down his purchases again this year.

When Fred arrived at the general store in O'Brien, a man of fine stature was visiting with Squire Sage. Clearly, this was a man of style, confidence, and wealth. The man wore a wool Derby hat. His frock was black with a satin covered collar, and he wore a wide, elaborate cravat of the latest fashion. A subtle satin stripe ran down the sides of his trousers. The man leaned on his cane, tapping his leather Congress boots with elastic on the sides on the wooden floor, as if wanting to attract attention to his fashionable (the newest) clothing.

Squire Sage introduced the man as Archibald Murray.

Archibald shook Fred's hand and seemed very pleasant. He said, "I came here in 1860, and I have been the county judge, surveyor, sheriff, recorder, treasurer, and auditor. I live in the house at the end of the street and I have a farm just south of here."

It did not occur to Fred that Archibald came here in 1860 and was probably one of the scheming men that Hannibal had mentioned. As time went on, Archibald and Fred took a great liking to each other and became fast friends.

Squire Sage wrote down Fred's purchases, and Fred left to plow and plant his second crop. Fred kept busy plowing, planting, and repairing a leaky roof and broken fence.

In the fall Fred made his second trip to Peterson and sold his wheat at the Kirchner Mill. On his way back he passed through O'Brien to pay his debt at Squire Sage's General Store. Fred had not been to O'Brien since spring. When he arrived in the village, he saw people gathered around a man they called Jake Waggoner, who was livening up the village by playing his fiddle.

Many homesteaders heard of O'Brien County, the rich soil, and the business opportunities in the village of O'Brien. Clark Green arrived and opened a second general store in one end of Archibald Murray's house. Chester Inman built a hotel and Daniel Inman built a blacksmith shop. A.H. Willets owned and operated the O'Brien Pioneer newspaper and had been appointed to Clerk of Court for the county. Fred could not believe how O'Brien had grown since spring.

A friendly man introduced himself to Fred as Frank O. Radeke. He said, "I am a friend of A. H. Willets, owner of the newspaper, who told me you are Dutch Fred. I live about a mile south of you, just over the Cherokee county line. I can see your smoke from my cabin." Fred was surprised that he had a neighbor other than the Waterman's.

A new court house had been built and Archibald Murray was using the old court house as his office. Fred was eager to visit with Archibald and stepped into his office.

Archibald told Fred of his latest venture. "I travel often and just returned from the Crawford County fair at Denison, Iowa. While I was there, I purchased a new invention to harvest wheat called a threshing machine. I brought it here, but I do not know how to operate it. Gus Baker, David Watts, and Hank Smith are young and curious. I have hired them to run the new-fangled machine. They will be harvesting my crop at my farm tomorrow if you would like to watch. I will be charging a small fee to harvest other people's crops."

It was a hot August day as Fred traveled to Archibald Murray's farm to watch the new invention. Not realizing the danger of the newfangled machine, Fred stepped closer and closer to watch it work. He stepped so close that his smock became tangled in a cog wheel, nearly pulling him into the machine and death. The young workers pulled with great effort to free him, ripping his smock as they pulled him away from the machine.

Fred looked at his torn smock and stated, "I make him too stout." The men laughed, but knew they were very fortunate to have saved Fred's life.

TWELVE
Hard Times

Fred could see that the land was being taken up rapidly. He would have to file on his land before someone jumped his claim.

On August 22, 1868, Fred was in the United States land office at Sioux City, Iowa to file a homestead claim on eighty acres of land in the northwest quarter of section thirty four, Waterman Township, in O'Brien County.

Fred stepped up to the clerk at the land office and stated that he wanted to file homestead papers. The clerk, a short mousey woman, asked, "Do you have a Declaration of Intent stating that you have lived in America for at least two years? You cannot file homestead papers without it."

Fred took the paper for which Mr. Lampton had helped him apply from his smock and handed it to the clerk. He could see the clerk was surprised when he produced the official paperwork. He remembered that he had wanted to leave Cleveland without filing for the Declaration, but Mr. Lampton had insisted and went to the county court with him.

The clerk said, "You will have to live on your claim five years before it belongs to you. It will be yours August 22, 1873. At that time return to Sioux City and change the papers from "homesteader" to "owner."

Fred was content that his homestead would be his in five years. He thought of Wilhelmine and wondered if she would travel to America to be with him. He knew that August Kolbus was the guardian of Wilhelmine, Sophie, and Anna Marie, and wondered if he would let them leave for America. Alas, he knew even if August released them, they would not have money to purchase supplies and passage tickets. If Wilhelmine had saved the two dollars that he had sent her, it would not be enough, and he did not have money to send her now. Everything he earned went to pay his debts. Sadness overwhelmed him as he realized he would never see them again.

Another year passed and fall arrived along with swarms of locusts moving across the land, destroying wheat, and all that was in their path. Frank Radeke rushed to Fred's soddy. The locusts had already destroyed Frank's crops, and he wanted to warn Fred of the disaster, but it was too late. The men stood in silence, staring at the swarming locusts as they ate their way through Fred's wheat.

There would be no crop to sell and no money to purchase supplies. Fred could not help but think that he would have had his wheat harvested if he had hired Archibald Murray to harvest it with his new threshing machine.

The settlers were all struggling to re-establish their homesteads. They could not afford to buy poles and firewood from Fred. Fred fell into depression. He could not pay his debt, and any hope he may have had of seeing Wilhelmine and Sophie was gone.

The farmers all traveled to O'Brien for supplies, but Squire Sage would not give them credit as they were still indebted to him. Fred and others went to Mr. Green's General Store and asked for credit until their next crop could be harvested. Mr. Green needed the business and gladly wrote down their supplies.

Everyone knew that with winter soon to arrive and no crop to sell they would have to hunt, gather nuts, berries, and catch fish to preserve with salt. It would be a long winter.

Throughout winter Wm. and Ed continued to stop at Fred's soddy for coffee and warmth. After a time Fred no longer drank coffee with them and he brewed the coffee unbearably weak. Eventually he did not have coffee to brew or food to offer them. Warmth was all he had to offer.

Wm. knew Fred was unable to purchase supplies and told him, "We are on our way to Cherokee to sell furs and we will purchase supplies for you."

"I do not have money to pay you," Fred explained

"You can pay me next year when you sell your crop."

Trapping was a lucrative business and Wm. and Ed had become very wealthy.

On October 26, 1868, Wm. wrote on a piece of paper that he had purchased coffee for Fred. On October 31st, Wm. wrote that he loaned Fred six dollars. November 28th, Wm. loaned Fred five dollars cash and bought him coffee, tallow, tobacco, meat, and boots.

Wm. smiled and said, "There are holes in your boots and the soles are falling off. Your feet must be cold. You will not be able to wear those old boots through another winter." Fred looked down at the worn and holey boots that he was wearing when he left Prussia. He thought of the time he gave George his extra pair of boots and trousers that he had carried in his trunk across the ocean to Cleveland.

February 1, 1869, Wm. bought coffee and soap for Fred. April 22 he purchased tobacco, and loaned Fred one dollar cash. Fred owed Wm. twenty three dollars and five cents for the winter purchases.

Wm. asked Fred if he would help them trap. "I will give you credit on your account." Fred had never trapped before, but he was willing to learn and helped several times. Wm. gave him seven dollars credit.

Fred crossed the river many times a day to check William's traps. Crossing the river was a tedious job, and he was pleased to see a ferry boat being built the next year. The Jenny Whipple was an odd looking boat. Her sides were straight up and the ends sloped out. The deck was five feet longer than the bottom, making her very unstable. Anything crossing on the Jenny must stay in the middle, but it was difficult to keep oxen from moving around. A stranger was once crossing on her when his oxen moved, tipping the Jenny on her nose and sending the oxen, the stranger, and the captain into the river. In 1871, the Jenny Whipple was put out of commission and used to support a pontoon bridge. An iron bridge was erected in 1872.

Fred worked hard to save his homestead, but living in America had not been good for him. The soil was black and rich and there were trees, but locusts and drought plagued all the homesteaders. Fred's poles did not sell, and each year his debt grew. Hannibal Waterman hired Fred to help him with various jobs, and paid him in January of 1873. Fred traveled to O'Brien to pay his debt and purchase supplies. Upon arriving in O'Brien, Mr. Green told Fred that Archibald Murray had died. Fred was devastated and wanted to know when he would be buried, but he had already been buried in a small cemetery on the Waterman homestead.

Fred returned to the Waterman property and found the small cemetery. Four Waterman sons, Archibald Murray, and a Civil War veteran, Luther Head, were named on markers along with fourteen unmarked graves. Fred knelt and wept as he read the names on the markers. He felt alone and sorrow overtook him. He did not know the Waterman's had lost four children . . . all sons.

A weathered and broken stone marks the burial of Orran and Leon Grant Waterman

Orran S. Waterman
Aged 10 yrs. & 2 mos.
Died Dec. 3, 1871

Leon Grant Waterman
Born Oct 5, 1868
Died May 6, 1870, 1 year 7 mos.

Children of H.H. & H.H. Waterman

Son-not named
Age 3 weeks
Died May 14, 1859

Stillborn Son
of Mr. & Mrs. H.H. Waterman

Archibald Murray
May 17, 1830
Jan 5, 1873

Luther E. Head
p v t
8 N.H. Inf.
September 21, 1872

Archibald Murray's remains would eventually be moved to the Peterson cemetery.

Sorrow hung heavy in Fred's heart and he could not bear the thought of living. He had left his wife and child in Prussia, and all of his friends were left behind him. America had not been the answer to his dreams, and he was tired of the struggle to save his land. He no longer wanted to be alone or live.

His depression grew deeper and on February 4, 1873, Wm. and Ed found Fred sick in his soddy. He told them, "I am going to die, and there is no use calling a doctor or giving me medicine. I have a daughter in Prussia whose name is Marie Sophie Feldman. Please see to it that she is given my land and possessions. I would like to be buried beside Archibald Murray in Hannibal Waterman's cemetery." Fred seemed to be a fatalist and had given up.

Wm. and Ed gave Fred kind and gentle care, and then took him to Cherokee County to the home of his neighbor Frank O. Radeke. Fred demanded that Mr. Radeke not call a doctor, but Mr. Radeke went against Fred's wishes and secured the service of Dr. M.S. Butler, a pioneer physician of great skill and ability, residing in Cherokee. Dr. Butler made three trips to attend Fred's sickness on February 7, 9, and 11. Dr. Butler stated that the patient did not seem to desire to live and was not helping himself as he might.

Without fear or trembling on February 13, 1873, Frederick Wilhelm Feldman, known to all in O'Brien County as Dutch Fred, passed on to the great beyond.

In the presence of two score friends and neighbors, D. W. Young, a neighbor and lay man, preached the funeral sermon. A quartet of ladies furnished the music and sang hymns. Fred's request to be buried beside Archibald Murray was not honored. He was buried in the valley of his homestead with no headstone to mark his life. Fred had lived on his homestead four and one half years, six months short of completing the requirements for title.

His administrators were unable to secure an heir living in America to continue the patent and the land was lost.

THIRTEEN
The Facts

A.H. Willits, Clerk of Court for O'Brien County, owner of the O'Brien Pioneer newspaper, and friend of Frank O. Radeke, appointed administrators to Fred's estate on February 15, 1873, two days after his death.

Willits authorized the administrators to appraise and sell Fred's belongings as soon as possible. On February 21, 1873 the administrators ran this ad in the O'Brien County Pioneer newspaper, stating as is:

> **Administrator's Notice**
> **Notice is hereby given that the undersigned was on the 15th day of February A.D. 1873 duly appointed and qualified by the Circuit Court of the State of Iowa in and for the O'Brien County, as Administrators' of the estate of Fred. Feldman. Late of said county dec'd, and all persons having claims against said estate are requested to file the same duly authenticated with the undersigned Administrators' and all persons owing said estate will make immediate payment to:**

WILLIAM S. FULLER, JOHN W. BROCKSCHINK, FRANK O. RADEKE, Administrators'

Bills in the amount of $149.25 were turned in against Fred's estate. Wm. Baker, Frank O. Radeke, and Dr. M.S. Butler submitted these bills to Fred's estate.

Fred Feldman

In acct-with Wm. Baker

Oct-26th 1868	Coffee		1.00
31st	Cash		6.00
Nov 28th	Coffee		1.00
	Cash		5.00
Tallow & Tobacco			.70
	Meat		.50
	Boots		6.50
Feb 1st /69	Coffee		1.00
	Soap		.15
April 22	Tobacco		.25
	Cash		1.00
	Total		$23.05
	Paid in work		-7.00
	Balance Due		16.05 "

Feb. 20, 1873 Radeke purchased a coffin for $18.00

from "W. Pelton-Dealer-in all kinds of furniture," Cherokee, Iowa.

May 7, 1873 Radeke turned in a bill to the estate that included a charge of $30.00 for a coffin

Frank O. Radeke against F. Feldman Estate for taking care of Fred Feldman while sieck (sick) at my house from Feb 4th until Feb. 13 and gitin (getting) close (clothes)

Coffin			$30.00
1 shirt			1.00
1 Henkerchief (Handkerchief)			.50
1 Pire (pair) Drawers			.75
Don (done) work after his death			
Feb 13 Haling (Hauling)	½ day		1.25
"18"		1 day	2.50
"20"		1 day	2.50
"25"		½ day	1.25
Making in Full			$42.25

Dr. M.S. Butler
State of Iowa   The Estate of Fred Feldman Dec'd.

Cherokee, Iowa May 13-1873   being duly sworn on oath say that the foregoing
                             for medical services was made during the last
Professional Visits   sickness of said Feldman, Deceased, and that the
Feb 7, 1873 $7.00   same is just and true and no part thereof has been
Feb 9, 1873   7.00   paid. M.S. Butler
Feb 11, 1873   7.00
Total $21.00

Dutch Fred's administrators listed two pages of inventory, which included; six hundred rails, four hundred and fifty stakes, eight logs, a stable, a pig, forty-four chickens, one yoke of big, red oxen, a wagon, two old plows, a pair of boots, one gun and powder horn, and many other articles. These are some of the items that were sold:

1 yoke of big, red oxen sold to W.W. Mores	$85.00
600 rails and poles to E. McClinton	24.00
Two old breaking plows to Dice	5.00
8 chickens to Willits	1.60
Stable to Smith	15.00
One gun and powder horn to E. Robinson	1.00
1 pair of boots to J. Manly	.75
1 scythe to Ed C. Brown	2.50

Fred's precious knife was not listed among his inventory. Slowly his belongings were sold and on October 6, 1873 the last item to sell was the wagon that had carried Fred to northwest Iowa. It was sold to a man named Kolle for $6.00. The inventory sold for a total of $237.30.

C. L. Stearns turned in a late bill for $10.00. Administrators W.J. Fuller and Frank O. Radeke were each paid $15.00; Administrator J.W. Brockschink was paid $10.50; $5.00 was unaccounted for in the estate record. It was stated by the Administrators that $32.55 was left for the guardian of Marie Sophie Feldman.

The estate was kept open until proof of heirship could be established by Marie Sophie in Prussia. On April 25, 1879 Franz Heinrich and Christian Hanau, both of Espelkamp, Prussia, signed a letter that was drawn up by Judge Weihe of the Royal Prussian Court of Appeals, and sent to the court at Primghar, Iowa, stating that they knew Fred, Wilhelmine, and their daughter Marie Sophie.

The letters read as follows:

April 25, 1879

> Frederick Wilhelm Feldman of Espelkamp, who immigrated to America about 14 years ago (1864), was known to me. Our neighborly intercourse which we kept up with each other enables me to give full information about his personal affairs. He married with Wilhelmine, maiden name, Eilers, from whom he was afterwards separated by divorce. One child was the issue of this marriage, Marie Sophie Feldman, who is now about fifteen years of age, single servant girl. The said deceased Feldman had no other children out of this marriage, nor was he ever married either before or after his marriage with the said Wilhelmine Eilers.
>
> Franz Heinrich
>
> Christian Hanau

October 1, 1879, proof that August Kolbus was guardian of Marie Sophie was sent from the Royal District Court, Espelkamp:

To the American Probate Court,

For the county of O'Brien, in the state of Iowa, North America

Rahden October 1, 1879

It is hereby certified that the tenant, August Kolbus, of Espelkamp, as guardian of Marie Sophie Feldman at Espelkamp, is duly appointed administrator of the hereditary share of his ward and authorized to receive the same and to execute the power of attorney bearing date June 10, 1879, within special approval of the Court for executing said power.

We do hereby respectfully request the American Probate Court for the County of O'Brien in the state of Iowa, to order moneys due to be paid, and we likewise give assurance that in similar cases, in compliance with the laws of this country, payment shall be made to the guardian appointed in the United States

Royal District Court Weihe

August Kolbus, guardian of Wilhelmine, her mother Anna Marie, and daughter Marie Sophie, was paid $32.55 on May 14, 1880. The estate of Frederick Wilhelm Feldman was closed seven years after his death.

Fred never knew that Wilhelmine exchanged the American dollars that he had sent her in 1867 and saved those silver coins until 1869 when she used them to buy her release from August Kolbus's guardianship. Kolbus would not release her mother and daughter as he demanded more coins. Wilhelmine had fallen in love with a man named Christian Heinrich Knowles. She felt once she was married there would be money to buy her mother and Marie Sophie's release.

Christian and Wilhelmine married on August 4, 1869 and a daughter, who they named Sophie Louise Knowles, was born March 27, 1870. Another daughter, Wilhelmine Dorothy Knowles was born September, 1875.

It is unknown whether Marie Sophie and Anna Marie were ever released from August Kolbus's guardianship.

AFTERWORD

In 1881 the Northern Railroad laid tracks on the north side of the Little Sioux River and did not pass through the town of O'Brien. A depot would be built five miles northwest of O'Brien and the citizens of O'Brien moved to the thriving new village of Sutherland.

When a Civil War veteran, James P. Martin and his family, moved to Sutherland in 1886 they were told many stories about a quiet and gentle Prussian immigrant everyone called Dutch Fred. Hannibal Waterman enjoyed telling of Fred dressing as a Prussian field laborer, his smock sewn with heavy twine and hanging outside his trousers. Hannibal remembered that Fred had such a long name that he gave him the nickname of "Dutch Fred." Squire Sage chuckled as he told about Fred's big, red oxen that were hard to control, but Fred always managed to keep them from running over hitching posts and people. Wm. and Ed told about Fred's weak coffee, but they were always welcome at his soddy. Gus Baker, David Watts, and Hank Smith told the story of saving Fred's life when his smock became tangled in the newfangled machine. Mr. Greene told that Fred was buried in the valley of his homestead without a marker to tell that he had lived.

James P. Martin thought many times about the man who was buried without a marker. In 1922 James secured contributions of one dollar from each citizen of Sutherland to construct a suitable marker for Dutch Fred's grave. Roy Lampman, with the help of others, disinterred Dutch Fred's remains and James P. Martin furnished the labor to pour a cement marker.

The remains of poor old Dutch Fred were taken from the unmarked grave in the valley to the top of a bluff on his homestead, facing the Little Sioux River, and buried there. The monument bearing Fred's name still stands today overlooking the land he struggled so hard to find and homestead.

James P. Martin was born in Aberdeen shire, Scotland on November 10, 1847. The family immigrated to America in 1852. James and his four older brothers joined the Union Army in 1864 to fight in the Civil War. James died at the home of his daughter, Elsie Hill, of Sutherland, Iowa on September 20, 1949 at the age of 101 years, 10 months, and 10 days. He was Iowa's last surviving Civil War veteran. Today four Civil War swords hang in his honor at the Prairie Heritage Center which is east of Sutherland, across from the Waterman homestead, and one mile from Dutch Fred's homestead.

Fred's last name is not spelled correctly (Fieldman) on the tombstone, and January is listed as his death month, but official documents tell it is spelled Feldman and he died February 13, 1873. However, thanks to the efforts of J.P. Martin, "Dutch Fred" will be remembered for many years to come.

DUTCH FRED

Without fear or trembling on February 13, 1873 Frederick Wilhelm Feldman, known to all in O'Brien County, Iowa as Dutch Fred, passed on to the great beyond.

ACKNOWLEDGEMENT

My heartfelt thanks to family and friends, who read, re-read, made suggestions and contributed in many ways toward the completion of this book. Betty Taylor, Joanne Schar, Darla Bailey, Daneille Nelson, and Jaymee Logan. Special thanks to Dr. Tadd Knobloch DC, and Lila Kummerfeld.

Printed in Canada